THE COUPE

A Novella

J BARTELL

&

GINGER MARIN

For information contact:
contact@bijouentertainment.com

Library of Congress cataloging-in–publication Data.
ISBN 979-8-9855122-3-6

Book Design by Bijou Entertainment
Cover Design by Jeanine Henning

DEDICATION

Dedicated to those who seek redemption on the rough roads of life. To the brave souls who, amidst the roar of engines and the clash of personal battles, find the strength to forgive and the courage to rebuild.

And for every lowrider cruising under starlit skies and every muscle car roaring to life, this story celebrates the diversity of journeys and the power of second chances.

CONTENTS

CHAPTER ONE

THE LONG WAY BACK

The solidly built forty-year-old stood in the center of his prison cell and took a last look around. Paint was chipped and peeling, and a rusty ring at the bottom of the toilet had been patched with green paint. He ran his fingers along the walls, counting each notch. The paint chips and blotches would soon be forgotten, but the years-long stay was forever etched into his mind, as were the people with whom he spent them. Some had become friends, although too few; many were nameless nobodies; still others had become mortal enemies — *May those in the last group rot in hell.*

The man was escorted down a corridor, flanked by two burly guards. His clothing was ill-fitted on his muscular frame — standard issue prison garb for those who had nothing better to wear for when they got out. His footfalls echoed off the bare walls as he approached the receiving desk where he collected his long-unused personal belongings, including a small duffel bag. He tossed in his keys, a comb, and the pair of sunglasses that had been laid out for his inspection, but he pocketed the wallet after making sure his I.D. and money were still in it. A ten and four ones.

The guard at the gate pointed the way to the bus stop, where Luis Alvarez walked, then boarded a bus headed to Los Angeles just as rain started to fall. It would be a long journey, so he took a seat way in the back and put his duffel bag on the seat next to him. His hands were scarred, and prison tattoos on his wrists disappeared under his sleeves.

Two and a half hours later, an image of a white cross shifted in and out of focus in a rippling pool of rainwater as the steady downpour pelted it. The bus wheels smashed through the puddle as it passed a small church with a cross on its spire. Luis stared out the window, a vacant look that felt as dismal as the day.

The bus now carried a few working-class people, their faces etched with toil and trouble, on their way home from a long day of work. Luis noted the passing stores and streets, then rested his eyes briefly, letting the motion of the bus rock him.

A bell sounded and he opened his eyes — a passenger was already making his way to the back door to get off. As the bus stopped, Luis' attention was drawn to a broken-down neighborhood bar where a bouncer smoked a cigarette as he leaned against the building, sheltered from the rain by a short overhang.

From inside the bus, Luis stared at the bar, recalling sounds of the past — low salsa music, joyous laughter. Then the music grew louder and more frenzied as long-ago days seeped into his mind, turning the bar's exterior into a hot nightclub with a neon sign. He saw a younger version of himself exit the club amid happy, laughing people while a baby-faced man looked on. That was his best friend Miguel — drunk, his head thrown back in laughter.

Back in the present, the bouncer, annoyed by Luis' incessant stare, flicked his cigarette at the bus window. It landed right at Luis' face, but he didn't even flinch, his expression unmoved.

The bus moved on and passed a lowrider car, sleek tan with yellow and cream flourishes, that caught Luis' attention. His stop was approaching, so he reached for the cord out of an old habit, but found only a red button with the word *Stop*. As he pressed the button, his eyes stayed glued to the lowrider, as if memorizing every hand-painted line. After he exited the bus, the doors banged shut behind him.

It was a long moment before he could make his feet move. He turned up his collar against the rain and walked down a side street to a small, well-kept house. Luis stopped a moment to take in its miniature grandeur, the pride still intact, then moved to the door. He knocked softly, then a little louder when the knocks went unanswered. He then walked to the front window and, through the curtains, saw someone moving within. It was a petite Latina, neat in her appearance, her dark gray hair bundled in a bun, and wearing a house dress and slippers. She appeared to be about twenty years older than Luis. Of course, he recognized her.

Luis used his finger to knock on the window. The woman startled, then hesitantly walked over. She peeled back an edge of the curtain, peeked out, and saw Luis' hardened appearance. His lined face, scruffy beard, and straggled hair both frightened and confused her, causing her to gasp as she dropped the curtain edge and stepped back. All she could do was stare at the curtains, frozen between fear and disbelief.

Luis tapped the glass again as his face came closer to the window. "It's me… Luis."

She pulled back the curtain and Luis smiled, which softened his features considerably. She zeroed in on his eyes, then broke into a gentle smile as tears streamed down her cheeks. The woman then rushed to the door and opened it. Luis instantly lifted her off her feet while closing the door behind him with his foot. In Spanish, the woman said a quick prayer, "Thank you, God, for bringing my son back home to me."

Luis put his mother down, and she looked closely now at his worn face, and he at hers, taking in the damage time had done. Her hand rose to his cheek, her fingertips reading the story of each wrinkle and scar as if they were words on a page. He then kissed her gently as she cried torrents of lost tears.

After a moment, Mama slapped him hard across the face, shocking him. "That's for not letting me come see you."

"How could I let you see me in a cage?"

"All those years, Luis, and look at you now. You're a man when before you were just a boy." Luis suddenly realized he was dripping all over the floor, and Mama now noticed the water dropping from his clothes. "Luis, go change into something dry."

He moved off down the narrow hall to his old room, and Mama's legs weakened. She collapsed into a chair and tried to collect herself, pressing a hand to her chest.

In the hallway, Luis slowly scanned the photos on the walls: his baby pictures, high school graduation, Mama and his father's wedding day, Luis and his father under the hood of a car working, teenage Luis with a girl and his friend Miguel, all frozen versions of a life that had kept moving without him.

As he stepped into his old room, he was surprised to see that it was exactly the same as when he left — a young man's room. The walls were still lined with posters of sleek cars and shelves filled with gleaming trophies, auto magazines, and other paraphernalia. Somehow, the familiar scent of gasoline and oil lingered in the air, even after all these years, stubborn and unmistakable. Or perhaps it was just his imagination.

His eyes landed on a key hanging from a chain next to a photo on the wall. Luis took it down and clutched it tightly in his hand before glancing out the window to the garage in the backyard, its door secured by a heavy padlock. Suddenly, images flashed through his mind — screams, flames, a twisted metal frame. He forcefully shook off the memory and angrily tossed the key into the trash bin, the clatter louder than it should have been.

Stripping off his damp clothes, he took a moment to catch his breath and calm his racing thoughts.

Luis reappeared in the kitchen wearing a much-too-small sweatshirt and sweatpants. Mama looked at the poorly fitted clothes, shook her head, then left the room as Luis sat, looking at the coffee she made for him, steam curling upward. A moment later, she reappeared with a small stack of clothing that she placed on the table near him. He clearly recognized them. "You will fit into these," she said, as she lovingly smoothed the top layer of clothing, then sat to enjoy her tea.

"Thanks." Luis continued to look at the clothing, then cradled his head in his hands, overcome with grief, his shoulders sagging. "I should have been there for you when he died," he whispered.

Mama pursed her lips, then said calmly, "So, what will you make of your life now? What are you going to do? Do you know?"

Luis had a vague look in his eyes, the answer nowhere close.

"Your father always said do what you know best."

"That part of my life is over," Luis said as he moved off back to his room.

"Then, after seventeen years, you're still in that cage, Luis."

He lay in bed that night, listening to every creak the house made. His own body felt wrong in the quiet — too much space, too much stillness, nothing pressing in from either side.

Luis was half asleep as the sun peeked through the window and the hum of a sewing machine came from another room where Mama was working on drapery. He entered with a coffee cup, wearing his father's clothes, and stood watching her, unannounced.

"I do repairs for the dry cleaners," she said. "Money doesn't grow on trees, you know." Mama reached into a pile of clothes hanging across a chair and handed him a nice navy blue suit jacket. "Here, take this. Your father never wore it much. Sometimes he could be stubborn like that. I'll have some more for you soon. You'll need nice clothes when you look for work."

Luis noticed the new threading from the alteration while his mother repositioned the drapery on the sewing machine.

"But you take your time. When you're ready, the clothes will be ready too."

"I was thinking of looking up Miguel. You wouldn't happen to know where he is, would you?"

"Si." She kept on sewing as Luis waited expectantly. "He's working at Domingo's Garage."

Luis glanced out the window to where an old Volkswagen Beetle was parked on the side of the house. "Can I take the car?"

"If you can make it work, you can take the car. It hasn't worked since your father left us, and I don't have the money to fix it. You make sure you tell Miguel that I think he's a bum for never fixing my car."

Luis knew exactly where Domingo's was. Lots of kids from the old neighborhood had some history there, doing small chores and learning the trade. Miguel was one of them.

When he got there, Luis found his old friend wearing goggles and a face mask as he spray-painted the final touches on a lowrider car. Other men worked on nearby cars, but none was as cool-looking as Miguel's. "Bueno! You're some fucking looker," he said as he admired his own work. He then spotted Luis watching him. Miguel whipped off his goggles and mask and rushed over to him. The men embraced, and Miguel's eyes teared up. "When?" he asked.

"Yesterday."

Miguel scanned Luis' face, noticing the deep lines etched around his eyes and mouth, evidence of tough years and worry. "Holy shit, you've aged, man!" he exclaimed.

Luis chuckled, a hint of bitterness in his voice. "You think you haven't?"

Despite the smudges of paint on his face, Miguel still had the same boyish features that seemed never to age. His carefree attitude only added to his youthful appearance, making him appear much younger than Luis.

"Hey, I was real sorry about your Dad," said Miguel with genuine sympathy. "I went by your house a few times to make sure your Mom was okay and all."

"Thanks," Luis said simply.

Miguel checked the wall clock, then looked over to his boss who was working in his office. "Okay to go to lunch?" he asked in Spanish. The boss glanced at Luis, then nodded yes. Miguel turned to Luis. "Come on, let's get out of here."

They made their way to a diner just a block away and sat in a booth where they were soon surrounded by enormous plates of food — burgers and fries, plus all the fixings.

"So, what are you gonna do now?" Miguel asked.

"Why does everyone keep asking me that? I just got out for Christ's sake."

"Because that's what you're supposed to ask a guy who just got out, for Christ's sake."

"Well, I don't know."

"Maybe I could get you—"

"No!"

"You didn't even let me finish."

"I'll find something different."

"Okay, then, but if you decide different, let me know. Lots of places need good mechanics."

Luis sipped his coffee while Miguel slugged a beer. "Hey, did you hear about Rico?" he suddenly asked excitedly. Luis offered up a blank look, which disappointed Miguel. "No, I guess you wouldn't. Well anyway, Rico's dead. Boy, I've been waiting a long time for that to happen."

Miguel noticed his now-empty beer bottle and held it up for the waitress to bring another while Luis glanced out the window, his gaze drifting as if he were still adjusting to the flow of ordinary conversation.

"So, ain't ya gonna ask how the fucker died?" Miguel asked.

"Don't care."

"Well, this one I know you'll care." Luis looked back at Miguel. "Ricky Gonzalez. Are you ready for this? The guy's a doctor now!"

"No shit!" Luis was actually impressed with this bit of news.

"I'm telling you, he's a fucking doctor. And, get this, he drives a Corolla and makes house calls." Miguel paused as Luis picked through his French fries. "Hey, you eating them?"

Luis gestured for Miguel to help himself as the waitress dropped off a second bottle of beer for Miguel.

"Anyone else you want to know about? Yeah, yeah, I know you want to know. Okay, I'll tell ya. She got married."

Luis was unflappable. The one thing he really should care about — and yet didn't.

"Got a kid too. She didn't wait for ya."

"Why would she? I'm glad she found someone." Luis scanned the room. In an adjoining booth, a young couple was making fools of themselves while taking selfies. He got up and plunked down his share on the table.

"Don't get pissed at me!" Miguel said.

Luis hurriedly left the diner, which prompted Miguel to gulp the last of his beer, some of which dribbled down his chin and shirt. Outside, Miguel found Luis waiting for him. They headed back to Domingo's, awkwardly, as friends who've just had a tiff might do. "Hey, my girlfriend's got a sister," said Miguel. "She's not bad either. You wanna come out with us tonight to a new club? Get your mind off things?"

Luis wasn't exactly sure that was something he wanted to do so soon after getting out of prison, but he found himself agreeing. "Sure, why not?"

That night, salsa music boomed from the classy nightclub. A line of people stretched along the sidewalk, eagerly waiting for their turn to enter, while others were already inside, dancing and mingling in a haze of colored lights.

A flashy red sports car pulled up to the curb, drawing everyone's attention. Out stepped Sanchez, a 35-year-old businessman with slicked-back hair and an air of superiority, accompanied by his stunning Latina girlfriend, who exuded confidence and sensuality. She shimmied out of the car, her tight dress revealing long legs and a perfect figure. Sanchez straightened his glossy, well-fitted jacket before tossing his keys to the valet, who gave him a respectful nod — it was clear he had been here many times before.

The couple strode through the entrance with ease, completely ignoring the hopefuls in line.

Forget the 'No Smoking' rule, this place was on fire. Waitresses dressed in skimpy purple satin outfits glided through the crowd, expertly balancing trays of expensive drinks and hors d'oeuvres, as Sanchez and his date moved through the club like they owned it — because they nearly did.

Luis and Miguel arrived with Maria — Miguel's girlfriend — and her sister Zoe, both around 30, and found a table near the edge of the dance floor.

Sanchez continued to his own table on the second level where some of his cronies waited with practiced patience.

Miguel looked around. "Holy shit, this place is big. Must have spent some big bucks."

Luis looked around the lavish club, then up toward the balcony where he spotted Sanchez' daggered gaze fixed totally on him. Sanchez' eyes narrowed slightly, not in anger, but recognition — like he was placing a face he hadn't expected to see again. Without looking away from Luis, Sanchez whispered something to his captain, Julio, who was seated beside him — a big, street tough in a suit. Julio instantly pulled out his cellphone and made a call.

"Who the fuck is that?" Luis asked.

Miguel followed Luis' line of sight. "No idea."

Luis held Sanchez' gaze a beat longer, then looked away.

Maria tugged Miguel's arm. "Do they have food here?"

"No idea."

"I just want some chips or something."

Miguel flagged a waitress and pantomimed dipping a chip in salsa and eating it. He then half-pulled a vape pen out of his pocket for Luis to see and leaned into him. "Why don't we go out and have a couple of hits?"

Luis was taken aback by the suggestion. "Are you kidding? What part of parole don't you understand?" Disappointed, Miguel quickly hid the vape pen back in his pocket. "Sorry, man. Just trying to take your mind off things."

Luis couldn't help but feel irritated by Miguel's reckless behavior. "You come here often?" he asked sarcastically.

"Nah. We go to a little place on Third. We're only here because one of my customers gave me some comps as a tip."

Maria shifted her gaze to Luis, attempting to spark some conversation. "So, how was it in there?" Her curiosity was met with a sharp glare from Luis toward Miguel, causing Zoe to lean in and whisper to him, "It's okay, you don't have to talk about it." Luis visibly relaxed at her words, the tension in his shoulders easing, and the group settled into a comfortable silence while they watched the various dancers move to the beat. But Maria couldn't resist the rhythm for long. She fidgeted in her seat until she could no longer contain the urge to dance, her body swaying along as Miguel drummed the table in time with the music.

Zoe again turned to Luis. "Wanna dance?" She wrapped her arm around his. "Come on."

Luis tensed. "No, I couldn't."

"He's lying; he could always pick up the steps," Miguel said.

"Maybe later," Luis said, trying not to insult Zoe or himself.

Miguel then looked around for the waitress. "Where the hell are the drinks?"

"Okay, I'll just have to dance alone," said Zoe, who joined Maria in a chair dance as if they were kids trying to play with the adults.

Luis was again off the hook and simply took in the scene from a distance. Soon, the waitress appeared, juggling a tray of chips, salsa, and super-sized frosty Margaritas, which she set down at their table. Miguel quickly divided up the drinks, giving Luis the one with two limes on the rim.

"I ordered a Coke."

"This is a virgin, man. See, two limes! I know you want to stay cool," Miguel assured him.

After a few more drinks in them, Zoe, Maria, and Miguel took to the dance floor while Luis sat at the table, overloaded by the sights and sounds pressing in from every direction. It was a lot to process after years in the slammer. He finally got up and headed to the restroom, where he stood at the sink, splashing water on his face and neck, trying to cool down and calm his throbbing pulse. Afterward, he planted his hands on the sides of the sink, leaned into the mirror, and took a good look. He didn't know what to make of himself. He patted himself dry with a wad of paper towels and exited, moving back down the hallway that led to the main room.

Suddenly, Sanchez appeared from around the corner and forcefully collided with him. "You should watch where you're going," snarled Sanchez, a malicious grin spreading across his face. "You could hurt somebody." Julio and another one of

Sanchez' lackeys joined in, forming a menacing circle around Luis.

With tension pulsing through his veins, Luis held his ground and locked eyes with each of them in turn. He committed their sneering faces to memory, reflexively knowing that when trouble goes out of its way to find you, you'd better buckle up for a rough ride and hang on.

Nobody moved. Luis didn't speak, didn't shift his weight, didn't blink. He just looked at Sanchez the way a man looks at something he's already decided about. A long moment passed. Then Sanchez took a step back and tilted his head toward the hallway.

As he walked away, Luis could feel their cold stares burning into the back of his head. But he refused to let them intimidate him. With a steady stride, he moved on and out of the building entirely, leaving behind the three toughs and their toxic presence.

Miguel, half-drunk, exited the club looking for his friend and found Luis leaning against the side of the building, smoking. He gestured for a cigarette.

"Who the fuck is that guy on the balcony?" demanded Luis.

"Beats me. An ugly fuck, though. Why?"

"Nothing." It was obviously just Luis' problem for some reason he couldn't fathom yet.

He handed Miguel a cigarette, and his friend lit up, enjoying the taste and feel of the moment. "Just like old times, man," Miguel said.

Luis stomped out his cigarette. "I'm gonna take off."

"That's a long walk, man."

Luis gave a short wave of his hand and kept moving away from the noisy club. At that moment, he had had enough of the scene and Miguel. "Hey, don't worry, I'll take care of the—" Miguel continued, thinking about the bill. But just as Luis turned the corner, Julio walked by Miguel with a phone to his ear and his eyes riveted in Luis' direction like a locked sight. Not that Miguel noticed or, even if he had, that it would have meant anything to him.

Luis had walked a few blocks, lost in thought, when he stopped near an alleyway to light another cigarette. He let out a deep sigh and took a drag, feeling the warm smoke fill his lungs. Suddenly, the sound of clanking metal jolted him back to reality just as a car with three gangbangers jumped the curb and sped toward him. Reacting quickly, Luis leapt to the other side of the sidewalk, his heart racing with adrenaline. As the car flew past him, he rolled onto the ground to avoid being hit by its tail end. The bangers inside jeered and pounded the outsides of the car doors, their laughter echoing off the buildings as they drove off into the night. Cursing himself for not paying closer attention to his surroundings, Luis angrily flicked his cigarette into the gutter and quickened his pace toward a nearby bus stop without looking back.

He reached the bus stop and stood under the yellow light, breathing hard, rain starting up again. The car could have been random. Could have been kids. He almost believed it. Almost.

CHAPTER TWO

OLD STREETS, NEW RULES

The next morning, Mama had gone off to her seamstress job as usual, leaving Luis alone in the house.

He entered the kitchen, his muscular frame on display as he was shirtless. His chest, back, and arms were adorned with intricate prison tattoos, some faded but others still vibrant and carefully crafted. He braced his hands against the edge of the sink and dropped his head, rolling his neck slowly, the way a man does when he's working out a kink — except there was no kink. He was back there. Last night. The rain, the car, the way it had slowed just enough. He shook his head once, hard, as if he could rattle the thought loose. Then he looked out the window. The street was quiet. A neighbor's cat moved along the fence. Nothing. Nobody coming. He held it another beat anyway, reading the stillness the way he'd learned to read everything — carefully, and from a distance. Then he let it go.

With a sense of familiarity, he rummaged through the cabinets and found a jar of instant coffee. It may not have been the best option, but it would do in a pinch. He filled a teapot with water and set it on the stove to boil until it whistled.

Outside, Rosealia, the girl in the hallway photo with Luis, now in her mid-thirties and with a relaxed, friendly demeanor, came up the walkway, carrying two grocery bags that bumped lightly against her legs.

Luis' attention was drawn to a small radio on the counter, and he turned it on just as Rosealia walked through the door after using her own key. Startled by the sight of Luis standing in the kitchen, she let out a blood-curdling scream that sent groceries flying in all directions. Without thinking, she turned and ran in the opposite direction as if the house itself had betrayed her.

"Wait!" Luis called out after her.

But Rosealia was already halfway to the front door, calling out for Mama in a panic.

Luis yelled back, "My mother's at work."

Realizing her mistake, Rosealia stopped in her tracks and turned back towards Luis, who had now made his way into the hallway. They stood facing each other in stunned silence before being interrupted by the sound of a whistling teapot from the kitchen. Instinctively, Rosealia moved past Luis to turn off the burner while he followed behind her in a daze.

"I can't believe it's you," she finally said, breaking the silence between them.

"You look great!" said Luis, who was genuinely taken aback by how familiar she still felt.

"I didn't know you were home."

The couple's attention was suddenly drawn to the scattered groceries on the floor, and they both scrambled to gather them up and put them away. "I help your mother with the shopping," she said.

Luis couldn't help but notice Rosealia's gaze lingering on his tattoos. "Don't go nowhere," he said. He left the room while she continued to put things away. A few moments later, Luis reappeared wearing a clean, long-sleeved pullover, covering up his tattooed arms. He sat down and watched her as she neatly folded the grocery bags, admiring the way her delicate hands handled the task. The room was filled with a calm energy as they both took in each other's presence, a subtle tension building between them that neither of them named.

Another visitor was about to intrude on Luis. It was Miguel, clad in his stained work clothes, who made his way up the path towards the house. As he approached the door, his hand raised to knock, he caught a glimpse of Luis and Rosealia through the window. His body froze in shock and he slowly lowered his hand, unable to turn away from the intimate scene playing out before him in that quiet kitchen. Feeling like an uninvited guest, he backed away from the door, stumbling against a potted plant in his haste. With a quick reflex, he caught the plant before it could fall and alert anyone inside. A pained expression crossed his face as he stood there for a moment, watching Luis and Rosealia the way a man looks at an old scar he put there himself — before finally turning away and hurrying off, his fists clenched.

Back in the kitchen, Luis noticed Rosealia's wedding ring. "You got married," he said dryly.

"I was married... but he's gone now."

Luis looked surprised. "Why'd he leave?"

"He didn't. He was killed a few years ago."

"Oh, I'm sorry. Did I know him?"

She shook her head. "No one really knew him," she said with a hint of frustration. "I mean...oh, God, never mind." Rosealia's shoulders slumped, and she averted her gaze, folding her arms protectively across her chest as if bracing for judgment.

Luis could see that Rosealia was clearly upset and embarrassed over having to explain things to him. He wanted to ease any discomfort she was feeling. "Why don't you sit down?" he suggested gently.

But Rosealia remained standing, unable to face him. She offered up a lame excuse to leave, desperate to escape the overwhelming emotions that threatened to consume her. "Guess you and Mama have a lot of catching up to do," she mumbled, gathering her handbag and making a beeline for the door. "I gotta go."

Luis watched her leave, feeling confused but not about to stop her. It was a lot for him to take in too — the sudden appearance of his long-lost love and the mention of her having had a husband. He sighed and tugged at his shirt as if it were suddenly strangling him.

Later that morning, Luis pulled down the posters and other paraphernalia lining his room. He trashed most of it and packed a few cherished mementos in a cardboard box. He pulled a framed picture from the wall. It was Luis with his arm around a smiling, younger Rosealia, her long hair blowing in the wind, as she sat propped on the hood of a vintage 1939 Chevy Coupe. He put this photo and one with himself and Miguel, as grease-monkeys, atop his clothes bureau. Best friends for life, despite their current rocky relationship and whatever this new distance was.

In the evening, he hustled around preparing dinner, using every skill he learned in the prison cafeteria and from whatever he could remember from his younger days. Mama entered with a bundle of sewing in her arms. "What are you doing in my kitchen?" she asked with fake indignation. She watched him for a moment, then checked his progress. "It's been a long time since someone cooked for me." He kissed her on the cheek and she headed off to the sewing room, saying. "So what are you making anyway?"

"A surprise."

Just then, the phone rang. Luis wanted to get it but couldn't because his hands were messy with food. He tried to quickly wash them but Mama re-entered the kitchen and grabbed the phone. "Ola." She listened a moment then handed the phone to Luis. "It's for you. Some Maria person. Doesn't make any sense."

Luis wiped his hands and took the phone only to hear a lot of screaming and crying. He hung up, ripped off his apron and dashed to the door.

"What? What?" asked a shocked Mama, who then quickly attended to the food on the stove, making sure nothing was burning.

It didn't take long for Luis to get to where he needed to be. He barged into the same little neighborhood bar he had seen while riding on the bus. The second he swung the door open, Maria and the bartender exchanged a frantic glance before pointing over to a booth in the back corner of the room. His heart skipped as he saw Miguel with a sinister smirk across his face, gripping the bouncer's head back by his hair. Shards of a broken beer bottle glinted under the light as Miguel had it pressed just above the bouncer's Adam's apple. Photos of the bar as a fancier club in its heyday were on the wall behind them. Although, one was clearly missing.

"Say you're sorry. Sorry for everything," Miguel demanded of the guy.

The bouncer was barely able to speak with his head pulled back so far. "I'm... I'm... sorry."

Luis whispered to Maria, "What'd the guy do?"

"Nothing. He was just drinking with us when Miguel flipped out. He won't let him go. He's fucking crazy!"

Miguel bore down on the bouncer. "Say you're fucking sorry or it's over."

"I'm sorry! Please..."

As the bouncer choked out his words, Luis stepped toward Miguel, who began praying to himself. "Holy Mary, mother of God, pray for us sinners. I'm a sinner. Pray for me." And again, this time in Spanish, "Santa María, madre de Dios..."

"Miguel. Let him go." Luis motioned for Miguel to hand over the bottle. "You can let him go now. He said he's sorry."

Miguel shook his head no then said, "I saw you. You and Rosie. She loves you, man. She's always loved you. And I fucking ruined it for you."

"You're talking crazy. You didn't ruin anything."

"If I hadn't been fucking around that night. That's on me. That's always been on me."

"The past is done. Rosie's okay."

"No, man, she's all alone just like you. You don't understand."

"Understand what?"

Miguel's hands were shaking. "I saw you!" he shouted. Then he softened his tone. "It doesn't matter now." His breathing became more rapid. The crying was more frantic and uncontained.

"Just talk to me, man," Luis pleaded.

Miguel moved the broken bottle away from the bouncer's throat and aimed it at his own. Luis dove toward him, just barely knocking the bottle away, but it still sliced into Miguel, causing Maria to let out with a horrid scream. Luis then pushed the bouncer, whose face was twisted in fear and horror, out of the way as Luis applied pressure to Miguel's wound.

Paramedics and police officers, who had been called earlier, now rushed in and surveyed the scene. They made their way to the back at Maria's direction. A few crunched over a broken framed photo, the one missing from the wall. It was an exterior shot of the club, with a different bouncer holding the door open for Miguel and Luis, who were standing on the sidewalk next to a custom Chevy Coupe and waving at the camera. It was the same coupe pictured in Luis' hallway.

Miguel, his neck now bandaged and wrists bound by cold, unyielding handcuffs, was hoisted onto a stretcher by the paramedics.

Once the ambulance left the scene, Luis escorted Maria back home. The night's eerie silence was punctuated by their muffled footsteps and whispered attempts to unravel the enigma of Miguel's dangerous behavior but they came up empty. Eventually, Maria admitted to him, "I don't know if I can ever trust him again." Her voice trembled with vulnerability. She locked eyes with Luis, her gaze hardened by what she deemed to be Miguel's betrayal. With a terse, "Later," she turned and disappeared into the darkness of her apartment building.

Sunday rolled around and, at a small neighborhood church, singing filtered out, alerting passersby that it was indeed the Lord's day and time for self-reflection. Inside St. Mary's of the Angels, the congregation sat and sang along with the chorus of just three young girls. Mama sang softly as she sat with Rosealia, both dressed in their Sunday best.

The song ended, and Father McGuinn, a jovial middle-aged oddball, retook the podium to begin his version of a post-sermon chat. "I'm glad the rain from this past week didn't scare you all away. But you know what they say, you can't have flowers without the rain." He repeated it in Spanish, and some of the people laughed while the older ladies nodded in agreement. He continued in Spanish, pointing to one old lady,

"I knew you'd agree, you little angel you." The toothless woman laughed again.

Luis entered and stood just inside the door. He looked around and spotted his mother and Rosealia, but still kept back in the shadow of the doorway. Father McGuinn noticed the latecomer. "Hallelujah! Another worshipper. You're a little late, friend." He squinted, then recognized it was Luis. "Well, you know what they say... better late than never. Hurry up and find a seat before I run out of breath."

People giggled and Luis awkwardly found an empty seat as everyone watched his every move.

"You already missed the sermon, and it was a good one too. Everyone, this is Luis. Say hello to Luis."

The congregation chuckled and then replied like schoolchildren, "Hello, Luis." Mama smiled but Rosealia remained expressionless.

"Now, before I go to commercial, the thought of the day is forgiving. Remember, by allowing forgiveness into your heart, you will be letting go of the chains of anger and resentment that hold you back from achieving happiness and joy."

Rosealia turned around and looked at Luis who was staring at her. Meanwhile, the congregation nodded in agreement, while muttering, "Si... Amen... That's right."

"But wait, there's more. Give and so too shall you receive. And the Lord didn't mean just money... although money is always nice to receive, even though it hurts to give. And remember, money doesn't grow on trees. Everybody..."

"Money doesn't grow on trees."

"That's right. Now, a reminder that the Church is having a bazaar this coming week at the Cinco de Mayo celebration at the beach. We need volunteers to sell food and run the games and rides. Okay, that's it. God be with you and have a nice day today before a lousy day at work tomorrow." The chorus picked up a final hymn as people streamed out, anticipating their all-too-short, joyous day.

Outside, churchgoers filed past Father McGuinn, who shook hands, patted backs, and kissed kids on their foreheads. Luis, Rosealia and Mama exited and stood off to the side as McGuinn finished up with one couple. The priest then moved on to Luis and the men shook hands. "I see you can still take a joke," he said.

"I've always been the butt of your jokes," said Luis.

Father McGuinn then turned to Rosealia. "I'm sorry Bobby didn't make it."

She shook her head sadly and Luis looked quizzical. "My son," she explained. Something shifted behind his eyes — not suspicion, just the quiet adjustment of a man realizing the woman he never stopped thinking about had kept on living a whole life he knew nothing about.

"Don't worry," said the priest. "He'll get here soon enough. I feel it in my heart."

"I hope so."

Father McGuinn ushered Luis away with an apologetic gesture to Rosealia and the men walked around the parking lot.

"You heard about Miguel?" Luis asked.

"Yeah. I rushed down there but he was still so sedated I couldn't talk to him."

"I finally got a hold of the doctor this morning. That's why I was late. He said Miguel will be okay."

"Thank God. If you need anything, anything at all, you come see me." Luis gave a half-hearted nod. "You got some things rolling around in that head of yours, don't you?" said Father McGuinn. Luis shrugged. "Okay, that's fine. On another matter, Luis, I need a mechanic for some of the rides. Can you help us out?"

"Father, I really don't do that stuff anymore." Not eager to be engaged, Luis began to walk off.

"You don't want to be running away now, Luis. You know what they say. You've got to grab the bull by the horns."

"This isn't a bull."

"Seems like it to me," countered the priest.

At the hospital, the smell hit him first — antiseptic and recycled air, flat and institutional. Luis stood in the doorway a moment before stepping in. Miguel lay awake in bed, his throat heavily bandaged and hooked up to an IV and monitors, the soft electronic beeping the only sound in the room. Somewhere down the hall a cart rattled past and then it was quiet again.

Luis paced. He couldn't sit. The chair beside the bed felt too close to something he wasn't ready to name, so he kept moving, three steps one way, three steps back, his hands working at nothing. "What the hell were you thinking? You can't blame yourself for something that was my fault." Miguel tried to speak but couldn't. "Don't talk. Just listen." Miguel weakly shook his head no, but Luis kept at it. He stopped pacing and stood at the foot of the bed, looking at his friend — really looking, maybe for the first time since he got back. The bandaging at Miguel's throat. The way the IV line disappeared into his arm. The handcuff bruising still visible at his wrists. Luis felt the full weight of it press down on him, everything that had brought them both to this room. "Don't make what I did drag you down. It would kill me if I had to be responsible for you too."

Tears streamed down Miguel's face as he again tried to speak.

Luis moved to the side of the bed then. He didn't sit. He just stood close, close enough that Miguel could hear him without straining. "Rosie and me are okay. And whatever's meant to be at this point will be. The only thing you have to worry about is getting well." Miguel closed his eyes against the tears.

CHAPTER THREE

INITIATION

Later that week, at the beach parking lot, Mexican melodies flowed from the speakers at the Cinco de Mayo festival. Children squealed with delight as they rode the colorful carnival rides, and attendees strolled through rows of booths selling t-shirts and souvenirs. The scent of grilled carne asada and freshly made churros filled the air. In a designated area, lowrider cars with intricate paint designs and mechanical enhancements faced off against powerful muscle cars, showcasing their engine-revving skills. The proud owners meticulously polished every inch of their vehicles, from shiny chrome bumpers to hand-stitched upholstery, in preparation for the car show.

Inside one church fair booth, an open-air tent, Rosealia sat airbrushing flowers onto a house-shaped mailbox. On her table were flower pots and beautiful portraits of Mexican women in colorful dresses. All were listed "For Sale." One side of the booth had tables set up for a steady stream of diners, and Mama cooked nearby, efficiently juggling ingredients and plates. A bingo game was in progress in the back, where Father McGuinn was the caller. Many of the same people from the church were helping out.

Luis hurried in, disappointment etched on his face. Another business owner had turned him away, wouldn't even meet his eyes after reviewing his job application. But there, at the fair with the church group, faces lit up. Waves and hellos came immediately — "Hello Luis" came the now-familiar refrain. Luis offered a socially awkward wave. "What can I do?" he asked Mama. She tossed him a towel, indicating the grill, then caught Father McGuinn's eye and nodded toward Luis.

Father McGuinn came up to him. "How'd it go?"

"Just like all the others."

"I'll give Rodrigues a call. He's got a handyman service. And he's been inside," said the priest, indicating to Luis that the man he was referring to was also an ex-con. Clearly, he would understand Luis' dilemma and offer him a job without question.

Luis fired up the barbecue as Father McGuinn headed back to Bingo. Just then, Bobby, a snarky, rebellious high schooler, entered and crossed to Rosealia. "Mom, I need some money."

Luis eyed Bobby curiously. He'd spent enough years around young men headed the wrong direction to recognize the posture — that particular combination of swagger and hunger that never ended well.

"I gave you some yesterday."

"It wasn't enough."

Exasperated, Rosealia reached for her purse. "Don't ask again." She handed him a ten-dollar bill, and just as he was about to rush off, she said. "Wait a minute. What do you say?"

"Gimme more?" She playfully smacked his arm. "Thanks, Mom." He moved to leave again.

"Wait a minute. I want you to meet someone." She took Bobby over to Luis. "This is Bobby. Bobby, this is Luis, an old friend."

Luis shook Bobby's hand. "Hi."

Bobby reacted to Luis' strong grip, then said, "Yeah. Gotta go."

"Have a nice time. We'll see you later," said Rosealia, who then noticed that Luis was totally focused on Bobby as he exited. "What's wrong?"

"How old is he?"

"Just turned sixteen, Luis."

"Thought maybe he was older."

As Luis went back to grilling, Rosealia watched him for a moment, wondering what that was about, then continued with her own work. "Sometimes I feel like I'm just treading water with him, waiting for the big shoe to drop. Gangs, drugs. All getting closer every day." Luis' expression didn't need to change much, but he had a knowing look on his face that he earned the hard way.

Father McGuinn rushed over to Luis. "Hey, Luis, go over to the Red Tent, would ya, and see if they can lend us an extension cord and hurry back. Bingo's on a roll!"

Luis left the church booth and crossed the grounds toward the Red Tent. Sanchez, the fancy dude from the nightclub, walked past him in the opposite direction with his younger wife and kids, who looked to be around five and six. He wore a sinister grin — which seemed to be his go-to look. As they passed, Sanchez slowed just a fraction, his eyes flicking over Luis. It made Luis' shoulders pull back, almost imperceptibly, the way a man's body knows before his mind does. He deadpanned Sanchez and continued on his way, passing a popular Latino band playing loudly and hot-pants-clad girls singing the hit upbeat song of the month.

Opposite the Red Tent was the car show area. Luis noticed the entrants as he entered the tent.

Proud owners of lowrider and muscle cars engaged onlookers while Bobby admired the elaborate artwork of one lowrider car in particular. As Luis exited the tent with his extension cord, he spotted Bobby and went over to him. He stood right next to him, but the kid ignored him.

"That's about 20 coats of hand-rubbed lacquer to get that kinda shine," said Luis, trying to get a conversation going.

Bobby moved to the next car and examined the paint job.

"See that detailing. It's all hand-done, no stenciling."

"Hmmm," said Bobby as if it actually meant something to him.

A loudspeaker squealed, "Welcome to the Cinco de Mayo Exposition Car Show. As we get underway, we have a little display called the Hydraulics Hula. Get ready, get set.

"Go, car number one!"

Car number one was a jazzed-up purple demon with an equally demonic paint job. Its owner hit the hydraulics switch, sending the car into front-end convulsions. Its rear end quivered before leaping up.

"Holy shit! You see that?" Bobby said.

Even Luis was stunned by the action as lowrider cars had evolved significantly over the years, far beyond what he remembered.

"Car number two, let's see what you can do," came over the loudspeaker. The second car's owner popped the switch and sent his car into a jig worthy of an Irish dance company.

"How the fuck they do that?" Bobby exclaimed.

A young mother, passing the tent with her toddler son in tow, reacted to Bobby's language by scowling and shushing him. Luis told Bobby, "You outta watch your mouth. There are little kids around."

With the lowrider cars getting all the attention, the muscle car owners revved their engines, drowning out the loudspeaker. A shouting match ensued between the two groups of car owners, each telling the other to shut the hell up and cut the engines.

"Okay, okay," the voice on the loudspeaker proclaimed, "this is supposed to be a fun family event. Come on, everybody, let's give all these car owners a hand."

The onlookers applauded, and Jimmy, a white 48-year-old ponytailed muscle car owner, spotted Luis. "Hey, Luis, that you?"

Luis looked over and recognized Jimmy who descended on him. "Jimmy!" he said, embracing him with genuine warmth.

"I thought that was you," Jimmy said. "You back into the action?"

"Nah. Just looking."

Jimmy called over to his girlfriend, "Hey, Cindi, look who's here."

Cindi, forever 39, a kooky blonde with big hair, popped up from behind Jimmy's car with a polishing cloth. In a flash, she ran over to Luis and wrapped her arms around him and hugged the life out of him. "Ahhhhh! I can't believe it's you! When did you get home?" Cindi quickly waved over Mario, a younger car enthusiast. "Remember that guy we keep talking about? Mario... this is Luis." She turned to Luis. "Mario's one of the best body men around. And he's only 20. How disgusting!" She laughed as Luis shook Mario's hand and smiled at the joke. They were *all* old farts now and Luis recognized that fact as much as any of them.

Bobby stood there silently, piecing together that Luis had once been somebody special in this world.

Mario said, "They got posters of every car with one of your engines plastered all over the garage. Nice to finally meet you. I was starting to think you were a ghost or something."

Jimmy pointed and told Luis, "Check out his car." Luis began walking toward the line of muscle cars, but Jimmy directed him otherwise. "No, the third one. Over there." He pointed to the line of lowrider cars and they all headed over to Mario's car. "Would you believe that was a rusty junker just a few months ago?" Jimmy said.

"What do you think?" asked Mario.

Luis knelt and looked down the side of the car. "Beautiful job. How does it perform?"

Cindi chimed in, "You're gonna have to come visit the garage to see for yourself."

They laughed, then Jimmy caught the attention of another old-timer, Big Huey, coming onto the scene. "Big Huey, guess who's here. El Maestro."

Big Huey waddled over with a big smile on his face as if someone had rung the dinner bell. Seeing Luis, he ran at him like a football tackle.

"Slow down, Huey," Cindi said, but Big Huey was already grabbing Luis and lifting him off the ground, bouncing him up and down.

The cheerful commotion drew in other car owners — familiar faces from Luis' past — now eager to greet him after all these years.

Jimmy saw Bobby's stunned expression. "You didn't know this guy used to be one of the best fucking car builders?"

"And the fastest in the quarter-mile!" reminded one of the old-timers.

"He was your age when he started," Cindi told Bobby.

"Oh, shit," said Jimmy, "tell the kid the Cobra story."

"Yeah, the Cobra story!" yelled another old-timer.

"Some rich kid rolls into a burger joint drive-in, where we used to hang out, in a brand-new Shelby Cobra," said Cindi. "Thought he was hot shit. He tells everyone he's there to challenge Luis to a race. Now remember — a Cobra was one of the fastest things on four wheels. Four-twenty-seven under the hood. A monster. They line up. They race. Luis beats him."

Jimmy jumped in, laughing. "Guy wouldn't shut up — kept complaining the Cobra was junk. So Luis told him he'd race again... but they'd switch cars."

Bobby stared at him. "You mean Luis drove the Cobra?"

Jimmy grinned. "Yeah. And Luis beat him with his own car."

"I don't get," said Bobby.

Everyone laughed.

"Sometimes, kid, it's the driver, not the car that wins the race," said Jimmy.

Luis suddenly realized time had gotten away from him. "I've got to get back. It was great seeing you."

"Make sure you come for dinner... soon! Oh, here..." Cindi pulled out a business card and handed it to Luis. "Ain't it cool? I've been branching out. I design everything from car frames to hydraulics."

"Wow, an engineer. Who would've guessed," Luis remarked with a smile.

She laughed loudly and smacked him in the shoulder. "Don't be a stranger."

Luis headed back across the grounds, and now it was Bobby catching up to him and trying to make conversation. "So, like, you were into this stuff? That's cool. Didn't know they did stuff like this in your day."

Luis gave him a look. "My day?"

"So, you win any shows?"

"Some."

"You win any money?"

"Some."

"So how come you don't do it no more?" Luis walked faster. "My Mom's got a old, junker in the garage but it doesn't work."

"Probably because no one fixed it."

"So, why don't you? I could use some wheels."

"Then fix it yourself. That's the rule."

"There are rules?"

"There's always rules." Luis took the extension cord back to Father McGuinn as Bobby stuck close behind him. Rosealia and Mama watched, surprised.

"Maybe you could just help me a little. We could be partners or something."

Luis handed the cord to McGuinn and then headed back to the grill. "I don't think so."

"You have to if you want to make it with my Mom."

"Watch your mouth." Luis looked momentarily as if he wanted to smack the shit out of the kid. Instead, he slapped meat on the grill harder than necessary as Mama and Rosealia continued to watch the dynamic between the two despite their words being out of earshot.

"I'll fix it myself, asshole." Luis shot him a "fuck off" look and Bobby quickly moved off, pissed.

"What was that all about?" Rosealia asked Luis.

"Nothing."

Rosealia held his gaze a beat longer than necessary, then let it go. She'd read enough in the set of his jaw to know pushing wouldn't get her anywhere.

Mama whispered to Rosealia, "It was something, all right. See, his veins are popping out all over."

The merry-go-round spun while others braved the dizzying heights of the Tilt-A-Whirl with shrieks of delight from its riders. The air was alive with music, coming from the Blue Tent where couples bounced to the beat on the makeshift dance floor. Nearby, families and friends gathered around tables or spread out on blankets on a large grassy patch. Children ran about, their faces lit up with excitement as they waved sparklers in the air, eagerly anticipating the grand finale of fireworks that would soon light up the night sky.

The day had been long and tiring for Luis, Mama, and Rosealia, and now they sat exhausted with their feet propped up on chairs next to the worn-out cooking area. Luis' apron was splattered with sticky barbecue sauce, a testament to his hard work and dedication. Rosealia's once meticulously styled hair now lay in a droopy mess while Mama wiped her glistening forehead with a hand towel as she tried to cool down in the warm evening air. For a moment nobody said anything, and nobody needed to. It was the particular quiet of people who had worked hard together and earned the right to just sit.

"What time is it?" Rosealia asked.

Mama checked the little watch that hung around her neck. She squinted at the small face before announcing, "Twenty to seven."

Rosealia jumped up from her seat. "Come on, we've got to clean up. The concert!"

She rushed around, gathering pots and cooking implements and stuffing them into shopping bags. Luis joined in, a strange grin spreading across his face as they worked together like a team again. But Mama stayed seated, getting up slowly from her chair. "Leave it, leave it. I'll do it," she insisted.

"Don't you want to come?" Rosealia asked.

Mama began packing things up in a more organized manner than Rosealia's frantic approach. "What I really want is to soak my feet and go to bed. You go and enjoy the rest of the night. Father McGuinn can take me home."

"You sure?" Rosealia pressed.

"Go!"

Luis removed his apron and gave his mother a quick hug. "Thanks, Ma."

Outside the fair booth, Rosealia smoothed her hair while Luis fixed his shirt. She then looked around for Bobby. "He was supposed to be back by now. Hey, what happened between you two, anyway?"

"Cars."

"Oh."

"You want me to look for him?"

She smiled with an appreciative nod. "I'll save us some seats."

Throughout the parking lot, streams of people rushed past Luis, all going in the opposite direction. A tee-shirt salesman offered his goods at half price, and kids with extravagant face paint chased forgotten balloons that clung stubbornly to car antennas or bobbed like awkward ornaments in the low-hanging tree branches.

Meanwhile, Bobby was at the far end of the parking lot, where he approached six hardened gangbangers in their mid-20s who were lounging atop a picnic table butted up against a light pole and smoking pot. Nestor, the leader, sat at the front edge with Joey, a small but dangerous-looking tweaker, and Skizo, a frenzied scumbag whose eyes darted around like a caged animal. A young boy, no older than eleven, sat on a bike nearby — already being groomed to take part in their illicit activities as a 'Little Yummy' — watching everything, learning fast.

"Hey, what's going on?" said Bobby nonchalantly as he walked up, hoping for an invite.

"What the fuck you doin' here?" Nestor demanded.

Bobby was taken aback. "Nothin'. I was just—"

Nestor looked past Bobby and saw Luis heading their way. "Great, you brought him to us," he sneered. Bobby's face was a mass of confusion as the bangers came off the table, ready for whatever may come. Nestor gave a nod to the kid on the bike, who recognized the sign and immediately took off like a shot.

Luis saw Bobby among the boys and, as he approached them, deeply inhaled the deliciously pungent scent of the pot wafting toward him. The smell took him briefly back to better times that ended badly. He then stopped and gestured to Bobby to come. But Bobby didn't move. "Your mother's expecting you," said Luis.

Bobby felt the others' eyes on him. "Yeah, so?"

Two of the bangers laughed. "He ain't got no mother," said Nestor. "You got the wrong guy."

Luis locked eyes with Bobby for a long moment, causing Bobby to squirm, caught between wanting approval and wanting out.

"What the fuck do you keep staring at, you ugly fuck!" screamed Nestor. "He's not interested. What are ya, some kinda fuckin' pedo?"

One of the bangers hawked a whopping spit onto Luis' foot. He didn't flinch; he just stood his ground and addressed Bobby. "You coming?"

"He ain't going nowhere."

"Let *him* say it."

The guys all looked at Bobby to see what he would do. "Fuck off, mister," Bobby finally said with as much authority as he could muster.

Luis waited a moment longer, hoping Bobby would come to his senses before this crossed a line. When that didn't happen, Luis turned to leave. One of the bangers threw part of a hamburger at his back. Luis kept walking, measuring every step.

Nestor turned to one of his guys. "Grab the kid."

Luis halted abruptly.

When he turned back, he saw Bobby struggling against crazy Skizo's tight grasp. Big man Nestor pulled back his jacket to reveal a deadly gleam of steel tucked into his waistband, but before he could get to it, Luis bulldozed into him with explosive force. He slammed Nestor's face into the nearby light pole with his left hand, causing blood to gush from Nestor's broken nose and the impact to reverberate through his bones. With his right hand, Luis gouged the eyes of another banger, using his flailing body as a weapon against the one behind him. Joey and another thug tried to take on Luis, but he swiftly broke one man's knee with a sharp kick and dispatched Joey with ease before either could react.

As Skizo released Bobby and raised his hands in surrender, Luis motioned for Bobby to come with him. But Bobby hesitated, taking a step back in fear of Luis as much as the others. "Suit yourself," Luis growled before walking away and leaving Bobby to face the consequences of his own choices.

At the parking-lot concert area, Rosealia sat in a fold-up chair near a decorated stage. Luis took a seat beside her. "You couldn't find him?" she asked.

"He'll show up."

"Yeah. He wouldn't miss this for the world."

As Luis leaned forward in his chair, eyes fixed on the stage, Rosealia noticed remnants of the burger that hit him on the back. "What's this crap on your shirt?" She brushed it off without pressing.

As the three girls from the church chorus stepped onto the stage, the energy in the air shifted. The music began to swell, filling every inch of space with its lively melody. Luis and Rosealia fell silent, entranced by the performance unfolding before them. The lights danced across the stage, highlighting each performer as their voices blended together in perfect harmony. At some point Luis' hand had found the armrest between them, close enough that his knuckles just grazed hers, and neither of them moved.

Afterward, fireworks lit up the sky, and their sparkling remnants slowly descended to earth. Luis and Rosealia looked up from their new position, seated together on the beach.

"So here we are," she said.

"Yep."

"Kind of a hectic week, huh? Just coming home and all that and... Miguel, of course."

"I still don't understand why he did it," said Luis.

"He changed after the accident. Well, we all did, didn't we? Except with Miguel, it was different somehow. I wished we could have stayed friends."

A loud burst of fireworks drowned them out for a moment, then Rosealia continued. "So why didn't you let anyone come see you? I'm just curious."

"It wouldn't have helped anybody."

"I kept hoping you'd get out early. Then, when I heard about what you did from Mama, I knew it'd be a very long time."

"What I *had* to do."

Rosealia put her hand on Luis' arm. He took it as he edged closer. He touched her hair, then her face, and whispered to her. The sound of his voice, the breeze against her hair, and the manner in which he lightly brushed her arm with his hand all felt impossibly familiar. "There wasn't a night I didn't lie in bed and think of you. We lived a lifetime together in my dreams."

His lips brushed against her face and neck. Rosealia was breathless.

They had been moving toward this for seventeen years. That night, they finally stopped fighting it. A thousand lost nights rolled into one.

CHAPTER FOUR
FAULT LINES

Some doors open slow. Others just kick in.

Julio and Bobby approached an industrial warehouse that loomed before them, its metal exterior gleaming in the sunlight. The barebones appearance was only a facade; inside, it was equipped with rows of phones and computer stations, separated by flimsy partitions meant to be quickly dismantled and reassembled elsewhere. Men and women bangers in their 20s and 30s manned the stations, their fingers typing away furiously as they worked diligently without looking up. This was Sanchez's main base of operations, a hub of activity and technology that kept his criminal enterprise running smoothly. The air was thick with the smell of coffee and sweat as other workers bustled about, their faces serious and determined like factory laborers, not criminals. From the outside, it may have looked like just another warehouse, but inside, it was a hive of busy bees, controlled by Sanchez and his team with ruthless efficiency.

As Julio walked Bobby through to the back office, phone bangers plied their trade.

"The police and firemen's widows and orphans appreciate your donation."

"Yes, the warranty is free. I just need your Amazon account number and password."

"Congratulations on winning your new big-screen TV! How would you like to pay for shipping?"

Sanchez lounged comfortably in his leather chair behind his desk. Nestor and the rest of the injured gang members stood meekly against the wall, their bodies tense and their expressions filled with fear and humiliation.

As Julio and Bobby entered, Sanchez' gaze flickered over to Nestor, a silent command for him to leave. Nestor and his group scurried toward the front door, but Sanchez gestured toward the back exit. "The back," he said in a low, commanding voice.

The gang members slinked out like beaten dogs, their spirits visibly diminished. Once they were gone, Sanchez turned his attention to Bobby. "Please, have a seat."

Bobby hesitated, eyeing Julio warily before finally sitting down in front of Sanchez' desk, perched on the edge of his seat, ready to bolt. The imposing figure of Julio loomed over him, adding to Bobby's nerves.

Sanchez tried to put Bobby at ease with a friendly smile that never reached his eyes. "So, I'm told you know him."

Bobby gulped. He glanced at Julio's hand resting on his shoulder before answering. "Who?"

Julio's grip tightened slightly, causing Sanchez to shake his head disapprovingly. Realizing his mistake, Julio quickly removed his hand and took a step back.

Meanwhile, Sanchez casually got up from his chair and moved around to the front of his desk, taking a seat on its edge, claiming Bobby's space. "Hey kid, just relax."

Bobby took a deep breath, trying to calm his racing heart. "Oh... I just met him."

"How did you meet him?"

"My mother. He's a friend of my mother."

Sanchez leaned forward, his demeanor becoming more serious and focused. "I want to know everything he does. Can you do that for me?"

Bobby nodded eagerly. "Yeah... sure."

"I hear your mother could use a better car. Would you like me to help with that?"

Bobby's eyes widened. "Yeah, that'd be great."

"Good. We have an understanding." Sanchez stood up and gestured toward the door. "You know the way out."

Bobby looked over to Julio then left quickly without looking back.

Sanchez then turned his attention to Julio. "I said have them rough him up. Not the other way around."

"He just showed up. Caught 'em off guard."

"Next time do what I fucking tell ya."

"So, what'd this guy do, anyway?"

"Just stay clear of him for now. And no one talks to the kid but me."

"Can you trust him?"

"Of course," said Sanchez, who laughed softly. "We're his family."

In a quieter corner of the town, Luis sat with Father McGuinn in the dimly lit church. The stained-glass windows cast colorful shadows across the pews and altar, creating an otherworldly atmosphere. Luis' eyes were fixed on the altar with a distant look, lost in thought and unresolved memory.

"Lighten up!" said Father McGuinn, breaking the silence.

Luis turned to him, hardly comprehending the priest's words. "What?"

"How you gonna move forward while still carrying around all that shit?"

Now, that was not what Luis was expecting. "What?!"

"It was an accident, Luis. You gotta let go...that you were sent to prison, what happened in prison and everything you lost because of it." McGuinn's tone was dead serious for once.

While Luis pondered the sentiment, the priest decided Luis would need more time to process things and wanted to get on with the other business of his day. He stood and said, "Anything else?"

"What's the deal with that kid of hers?" Luis blurted out suddenly before he could stop himself.

"I know things were hard for you in prison but the world's a lot rougher than you remember it."

"Don't assume anything until you hear the sound of that door clanging shut behind *you*. What am I supposed to feel sorry for him? There've always been gangs."

"Feel sorry for them?" McGuinn's voice went flat. "This is war. You save the ones worth saving and throw away the rest." He looked directly at Luis. "I haven't thrown that one away yet."

"Is that what God's saying these days?" Luis scoffed.

"He would if he were down here in *these* streets," McGuinn replied as he handed Luis a leaflet before walking away.

Luis stuffed it in his pocket without reading it. Just more bullshit, he thought.

Later that day, while Luis was changing shirts, he felt the leaflet in his pocket and opened it to see McGuinn's *Words of Wisdom*. #1. *For the bake sale, put more chocolate in everything.* That put a smile on Luis' face. He was just about to close up the leaflet when he spotted #2. *Yeah, God says he helps those who help themselves, but why not bring someone else along for the ride?* It was followed by a few other pearls.

Feeling inspired despite himself, Luis gazed out the window toward the garage. The thought of what lay inside made him glance over at the trash can in his room. It was empty.

Without hesitation, Luis made his way to the laundry room. From a tool drawer, he grabbed a claw hammer and then headed to the garage. With one swift motion, he broke off the rusted hasp and flung open the doors. Dust danced in the air as sunlight filtered through the cracks. Along one side was a covered-up work station, tools and materials scattered haphazardly. In the back corner stood a car, draped with an old tarp.

Luis stood for a moment, looking at the dusty and neglected space before him as if measuring himself against it. Then, determination setting in, he stepped forward and began the arduous task of cleaning and organizing. Hours passed as he swept away years of neglect, wiping away dust and grime, storing misplaced objects and pulling old coverings from windows. The smell of the place changed as he worked — the dead air giving way to something older underneath, motor oil and metal and sawdust, the particular smell of his father's hands. Slowly but surely, the once-dreary garage transformed into a space filled with pride, potential and purpose.

Later, Bobby came up the drive and saw the open garage. He went in, ill at ease, and saw Luis piling boxes onto a workbench.

"My mom called and said you wanted to see me about something."

"Yeah, a job. The pay's fifty dollars a week to start. Take it or leave it."

"Fifty? That's it?"

Luis glared at him with his newly minted trademarked look that brooked no argument.

"What do I gotta do for the fifty?"

"Everything I tell you."

Bobby balked.

"I could find a hundred kids that would give their right arm for an opportunity to learn a trade."

Bobby stood weighing Luis' words against Sanchez. "Okay. Okay."

"First, be here on time every day. Seven o'clock."

"In the morning?"

"Of course, in the morning. You're on summer vacation."

Luis opened a box and pulled out some tools that he began organizing. "Every time you're late, you get docked five bucks. If you're late often enough, you'll be paying me to work here. You got it?"

"Yeah."

Luis turned to him. "There's no fucking around. No smoking, no drinking, no drugs, no gangs and no friends hanging around. This is a business. You'll work until I tell you to go home. You got it?"

"Yeah."

"Every time you break a rule, you're docked five bucks. Every time you give me shit, you're docked five bucks."

"You're some kind of hard-ass. Five bucks this, five bucks that..."

"You want the job?"

"Yeah."

"Start bagging up that trash over there."

"I thought we were gonna fix cars."

Luis pulled a tiny pad and pencil from his shirt pocket and made a note. "What's five from fifty?"

"Forty-five."

"That's what you got coming to you on Friday."

Exasperated, Bobby headed to the trash pile, mumbling to himself.

"What'd you say?" Luis asked, ready to make another notation on his pad.

"Nothin'."

Hours later, Mama and Rosealia returned from their grocery trip, their arms laden with bags filled with fresh produce and pantry staples. As they made their way up the driveway, they noticed the open garage door and gasped in shock.

"Oh my God, someone broke in," Mama exclaimed, her heart racing as she feared the worst.

But then Luis appeared, carrying a tool bag and smiling. "A beautiful day, huh?" he greeted them before heading over to Mama's Volkswagen to fix whatever issue she was having under the hood.

Rosealia stared open-mouthed while Mama's face lit up with joy. Luis was back!

Bobby exited the garage, lugging two heavy trash bags and wearing a sullen expression. He barely acknowledged his mother and Mama with a simple "hi" before disappearing back inside for more trash.

The women followed him into the garage and found a completely transformed space. The back window was open, letting in fresh air. It was so much brighter and cleaner. The work station was now uncovered, a mechanic's dream filled with every tool in its proper place. But the covered-up car remained just that.

The following day, Mama sat at the worn kitchen table with a stack of crumpled bills piled in front of her. Luis and Rosealia, sitting across from her, couldn't help but stare in shock at the amount of money before them. Three thousand eight hundred fifty dollars to be exact.

"It took years to save this," Mama said, her tone heavy with both pride and caution. "And you know, it doesn't grow on trees."

"Ma, I can't let you do this," Luis finally spoke up, his heart racing with conflicting emotions. "I only opened up the garage to give it a try, but all this money...there are so many things that can go wrong."

Mama reached out and gently placed her hand on Luis'. "But it doesn't mean you shouldn't try," she said firmly. "I've always believed in you. Now you need to believe in yourself."

Luis glanced over at Rosealia, who was on the verge of tears. She nodded encouragingly, taking his hand in hers for support. The room fell silent as they all held their collective breaths.

Finally, Luis turned back to the money, his mind racing with possibilities. "I could use some new equipment, parts," he said slowly, mentally calculating the expenses. "We'll have to spread the word that we're in business."

Rosealia smiled at Luis as she and Mama both were relieved. "Thank you for giving Bobby a chance," she said.

"It's good that a man has his own business," Mama added. "Your father would be proud that you're carrying on his." Luis put his hand on hers in a gesture of comfort and thanks for getting him back on track.

"I hope now you'll be fixing that ugly bug out there," Mama said.

"What about that old junker of mine that Bobby's been bugging me about?" Rosealia asked.

Luis nodded as if he were mentally adding it to his to-do list. "I'll check it out."

Later at the hospital, Luis and Rosealia stood in the bright, sterile hallway outside of Miguel's room. The sound of muffled conversations and beeping machines filled the air as they spoke in hushed tones with the counselor about Miguel's current mental state. Luis was carrying a flower pot decorated with bright colors and patterns, courtesy of Rosealia.

"He's not doing well today," said the counselor with a heavy sigh. "Found out he was let go from his job after things were starting to look up. Nice flowers, though."

"How much longer does he have to stay here?" Rosealia asked.

"Another day or so. But I'll want to see him twice a week after that."

"I think I have some good news for him," Luis interjected carefully.

"Well, he could certainly use some."

Miguel was lying in bed, medicated but awake, when Luis and Rosealia entered his room. Luis put the flower pot on a table next to his bed in the hopes it would cheer him up, but Miguel stared at it as if an alien spaceship had just landed and forgotten why it was there.

Luis and Rosealia took seats on opposite sides of his bed. "I have good news for you," said Luis.

Miguel's head drooped in Luis' direction. "He fired me."

"It's wonderful news," Rosealia offered gently.

Clearly unconvinced, Miguel's head now flopped in her direction. "He fucking fired me."

"You and me, compadre," added Luis. "Just like we talked about. A business of our own. We start small at my old man's shop, then we get a better place later."

Miguel's head bobbled as if trying to make sense of it all through the haze. He told Rosealia, "Maria's gone."

"It's true. He needs you," she said.

Miguel looked back at Luis as Rosealia's words finally sank in. "Our own business? Like real partners?" He looked back at Rosealia for affirmation, and she nodded. With tears in his eyes, he again looked back at Luis. "You mean it?"

Luis smiled, but Miguel's face suddenly dropped as another thought surfaced. "Oh. But I won't be around."

"The bouncer isn't pressing charges," Luis told him.

Miguel was afraid to be hopeful, so all he could do was stare at the window inset in the door to his room as if bracing himself for disappointment. A big smiley-face balloon was staring back at him, bringing an odd expression to his face.

Luis figured his friend was still out of it from all the medication. "We're gonna go. Get some rest."

Rosealia kissed Miguel on the cheek, then she and Luis made their way to the door. When they opened it, the suction drew the smiley-face balloon in slowly, almost ceremonially.

The balloon drifted in like it knew exactly who it was for.

CHAPTER FIVE

CROSSFIRE

Two weeks out of the gate and L & M Auto was open for business. Long enough to start thinking the worst was over.

The same old beat-up banger car, that had nearly hit Luis near the pulsing nightclub, now bashed into a trash bin on a dingy little neighborhood street. It was about 10 p.m. Inside were Nestor, who was driving, Joey, Skizo and Bobby. They were stoned, drinking beers and feeling almighty high on themselves as the thick smell and smoke from pot wafted out of a half-open window.

The car went down a dark alley, then slowed with its lights turned off as it approached the rear of a sex shop where a hooker was giving a John a blow job. Nestor let out a loud whoop in glee. When the pair noticed the car coming, the John zipped up, his fingers fumbling in fear, and the two scurried off in different directions.

Nestor then parked near an overflowing trash container a few doors down from the sex shop while the other boys laughed at having driven the pair away, drunk on power and stupidity.

"Fucker's gonna pay for not paying his monthly," Nestor declared, as he flipped two fingers at the sex shop's flickering neon sign.

"Hey, how many hookers does it take to change a light bulb?" Skizo asked.

"You mean screw in a light bulb, don't ya?" Joey said.

"Shut up," said Skizo. "This is my joke, asswipe."

Joey the asswipe countered. "Two. No, three."

"Two," said Bobby, whose phone suddenly vibrated. He checked it. MOM. He put the phone back in his pocket without answering.

"The answer is two," confirmed Skizo. "One to screw it in and one to suck-it. Get it? Suck it. Socket." Skizo laughed so hard he blew bubbles out of his nose with the beer. Joey and Bobby laughed lamely out of obligation.

"I got a better one," said Nestor. "How do you teach somebody to shoot and teach somebody else a lesson at the same time?"

They all stared, waiting for the punchline. Instead, Nestor reached under his seat, pulled out a paper bag, and handed it to Bobby. "Shoot up the asshole's sign."

Joey snickered as Bobby peeked in the bag. Shocked by what he saw, Bobby pulled back, his breath catching.

"Go on, take it out," urged Nestor.

"I don't think he knows what it is," said Joey.

"Yeah, I do."

"Show us," Nestor demanded as he pointed to the sign.

With shaky hands, Bobby carefully took the gun out of the bag and nervously aimed it at the sign. As he fired off one round intentionally, the recoil caught him off guard and caused him to accidentally fire two more shots, hitting the sign again and again until it finally fell down in a shower of sparks and glass. Bobby fell back from the power of the gun, which caused him to butt heads with Joey, who screamed "Asshole!" as he held his hand against his throbbing head.

Nestor laughed loudly before his phone rang. He saw that it was Sanchez calling and quickly answered. "Yeah?"

In the background, Joey tried to show Bobby how to handle the gun better, but their conversation was interrupted by Sanchez' voice coming through the phone. "You got him ready?"

"Yeah," Nestor confirmed eagerly.

"Good. Go have some fun."

Sanchez clicked off and Nestor turned to Bobby with a sinister grin. "Looks like you're gonna get some practice, Bobby-boy." With a roar of the engine, he sped off into the night.

Skizo cackled with glee. "Bobby's gonna bag a buck! Bobby's gonna bag a buck! Initiation day's here!"

Outside Luis' house, a vibrant bouquet of colored balloons danced in the breeze, tied to his newly hand-painted mailbox now glowing under soft lights. Lively music filled the air, growing louder toward the backyard, where a lively scene awaited. A beautifully crafted wooden sign, adorned with bright florals and illuminated by flashing white lights, proudly displayed *L & M Auto — Open*. In one corner, a group of Mariachis tuned their instruments while Rosealia and Luis bustled about, arranging an array of food and drinks on colorfully dressed tables.

Luis poured a glass of wine for Rosealia, who was aglow in her strapless summer dress. "Thank you for Bobby," she said. "I know he's a good boy at heart... well, of course I would. I'm his mother."

Her sweet smile egged Luis on to ask, "Tell me about his father. I mean if you don't mind."

"I don't know that there's much to tell. He was a good man. Owned a small shoe store. One day, he got in some real expensive sneakers, you know the kind the kids want these days. Some guys came in to rob the place and just killed him. Bobby was twelve. He wanted to know why his father didn't shoot them first."

Luis watched Rosealia closely as she took a sip of wine, his thumb running slow across his knuckles as if gauging what he would have done in that situation.

"I was just thinking about where we'd be right now if I hadn't—" said Luis.

"Don't do that," said Rosealia. "Nobody knows how things are ever going to turn out."

She smiled at him and Luis grasped her hand. "You know what's hard when you get out? It's trying to play catch-up."

Just then, Mama came out of the house with a large platter of food and Luis rushed to help her. "I got it," he said. He then turned to Rosealia and asked, "Where's Bobby?"

"I don't know. He's not answering."

Out in front, Mario pulled up in his sleek lowrider sedan, followed closely by Jimmy and Cindi in their powerful muscle car. The trio stepped out with Big Huey leading the way. Jimmy carried a magnum of Champagne while Cindi brought her best version of dessert and Mario clutched a rolled-up poster.

"This is the place!" Cindi announced just as another car pulled up with two other lowrider couples in their 20s. She waved excitedly, then everyone headed to the backyard, passing Mama's VW bug, another car and a van with the name of a band painted on the side: *Los Aztecas — Hot Sounds Traditional to R&R.*

There was no stopping Big Huey. He beelined straight for the food, grinning from ear to ear as he settled himself next to Mama.

"Yo, Luis!" Jimmy shouted. "Let the good times roll. Congratulations, man."

Meanwhile, Mario offered his words of encouragement in Spanish, saying "Buena suerte."

Amid all the commotion and chatter, Cindi suddenly let out a loud shriek. "Rosie!" she called out before dropping her dessert box on a nearby table and darting toward her friend. The two women embraced each other like giddy schoolgirls, exchanging kisses and hugs. "Oh my God, Cindi, you look great!"

Returning the compliment, Cindi beamed at Rosealia. "And so do you! It's been ages but you look even better than great! We've missed you guys so much! Oh...I even made a cake."

Rosealia's mouth contorted before she forced a smile. "No, this one is good...really," said Cindi. "I've been practicing."

Jimmy spotted the band. "Live band, huh? You're going all out!"

"Are you kidding?" Luis said. "I swapped a rebuilt tranny for this!"

The musicians were all set up and the leader gave Rosealia the thumbs-up just as the last musician entered, his extra-large sombrero pulled low, covering his face. That man stood behind the conga drums.

"So where's Miguel?" asked Luis while looking around.

"He'll be here," assured Rosealia.

A trumpet blast pierced the air, signaling the start of a lively new song. The drummer's skilled hands danced across the congas, culminating in a vibrant solo that drew applause from the gathered crowd. As the solo ended, the drummer lifted his head to reveal Miguel, donning a comically large fake black mustache. A wide grin spread across his face as he threw his hands up in victory, exclaiming, "Tequila!"

The attendees erupted into laughter at the unexpected twist. The real conga player then entered and seamlessly took over as the band transitioned into another tune. Amid the music and laughter, Luis shook Miguel's hand in congratulations while Rosealia captured the moment with her camera, knowing it mattered. Another one for Luis' hallway wall.

Mario walked up and unrolled his poster with a flourish. "Check this out." It read *Lowrider Super Show Championship, September 11-13*.

But Luis was focused on something else. He shook his head dismissively. "Nah, I got to get my business going. Can't waste time playing around."

"You build something really hot," said Cindi, "you won't have to go looking for customers. They'll be running to you."

Miguel nodded. "She's right."

Jimmy joined in. "I know you and Miguel can pull it off."

"Come on, we can do it," urged Miguel.

Even Rosealia added, "If you're going to have a partner, Luis, you should listen to him."

Luis furrowed his brow. "All we need is a car, and even for an old junker, that's expensive."

"What about my car?" asked Rosealia innocently.

"What kinda car?" Mario asked.

"A Chevy. I think a nineteen-fifty-seven."

"What model?"

"Bel Air."

Cindi's jaw dropped. "Oh shit! Your husband's?"

Rosealia nodded and Mario let out a low whistle. "That's a smokin' good year."

Nestor's car snaked around a street corner. Skizo was in back with Bobby, now blindfolded and holding the gun, his knuckles white. Joey sat in front, holding a large, stinky bag of something.

"Initiation day's here!" Nestor proclaimed joyously as they got closer to Luis' house.

Skizo guided Bobby's hand as he pointed the gun out the window.

Just then, Rosealia and Luis emerged from the backyard, hand in hand. Their faces were filled with pure joy and love. "It feels good to be happy again," Rosealia declared before Luis leaned in for a kiss.

Nestor slowed just enough to let Joey hurl the bag of wet shit that splattered all over Luis' festive mailbox.

Then GUNFIRE. Bullets shattered windows and flower pots, chaos erupting instantly. Rosealia shrieked as Luis pulled her to the ground. Jimmy's car took two rounds through the windshield.

In the backyard, tables and chairs were knocked over as partygoers hit the dirt. Jimmy shielded Cindi, Mario covered Mama, and Miguel froze momentarily, caught between shock and fear.

Bobby ripped off the blindfold and saw his mother and Luis on the ground. Skizo raised the gun again, but Bobby yanked his arm down and the car sped off.

Jimmy, Mario and Miguel ran out front as Luis helped Rosealia up.

"Jesus! You guys okay?" Miguel asked.

Jimmy saw his windshield. "What the fuck?!"

Cindi rushed to Rosealia. "I'm calling the cops."

"It might be the punks I had some trouble with at the fair," Luis said. Rosealia gave him a quizzical look.

"There's always assholes at those things," Jimmy said.

As the police sirens began to echo in the distance, Luis stood unmoving, veins bulging in his neck. Miguel watched him as the Mariachis quietly packed up and backed out of the driveway. One driver placed his hand over his heart when he caught Luis' eye as if recognizing something dangerous had begun.

In the backseat of Nestor's car, Bobby's and Skizo's fists pounded hard and furiously into each other's bodies for several blocks in a blur of rage and panic before the car came to a screeching halt. Nestor turned around and grabbed Bobby by the hair. "Hey, you wanted in, right? Am I fucking right or what?"

Bobby was still flailing at Skizo. "You didn't say anything about hurting my mother."

"I wasn't aiming at her," said Skizo, who smacked Bobby in the arm in an attempt to end it.

"Well, you almost hit her."

Nestor interjected, "We were just trying to scare the guy, that's all."

"Yeah? Well, why him?"

"It's none of your fucking business. You just do what the boss tells ya." Nestor then nodded to Skizo, who opened the door and shoved Bobby out. "You better think about whose side you're on because one day we might come cruising for you," Nestor warned as he peeled away, tires squealing into the night.

With things calmer back at the house, Mama and Rosealia worked together to sweep up the shards of broken window glass that crunched underfoot. "Mama, you've been up all day. Please, let me finish." Mama looked around at the mess, with dried tears plastered on her face, then relented and went inside without arguing.

Meanwhile, Jimmy, Cindi, Mario, and Big Huey emerged from the backyard, each carrying a heavy trash bag. The others who had come for the festivities were long gone. "That's about it, Rosie... anything else we can do?" asked Cindi.

Rosealia shook her head, unable to find the strength to speak. She was emotionally drained and could feel her body starting to give out after everything that had happened. Cindi gave her a tight embrace before saying goodbye and heading off. Rosealia slowly sank onto a porch step, feeling numb and overwhelmed.

The rest of the group bid farewell to Luis and Miguel, who were still hard at work nailing plywood over the shattered house windows. Bullet holes dotted the once-pristine wall like scars.

"See ya, man," Jimmy said with a heavy heart.

"Take care," added Mario.

Big Huey plopped next to Rosealia and gave her a hug before joining his group. They all piled into their cars and drove off, passing Bobby, who slinked onto the scene, keeping his head down.

Bobby saw his mother on the porch and ran to her. "Are you okay?"

Luis turned and walked over to Bobby. "How come you don't even ask what happened?"

Rosealia looked at Bobby, then Luis. "What's that supposed to mean?" she asked.

From his perch by the window, Miguel watched uneasily as Luis confronted Bobby.

"It was your buddies from the fair, wasn't it?"

"I don't know. And, they're not my buddies."

Rosealia got up. "What are you talking about?"

Luis ignored her and lit into Bobby. "What the hell do you mean you don't know? Were they getting back at you or me?"

Bobby squirmed. "I don't know. They don't tell me anything."

"Oh, my God," said Rosealia. "You knew this was going to happen? And you didn't say anything?"

"I didn't know. I swear it. Mom, you gotta believe me." Bobby teared up.

"One of us could have gotten killed. Oh my God. How could you?" She then turned to Luis. "Why didn't you tell me what happened at the fair?" Then back to Bobby, "Is that what you want to become like, those criminals who killed your father?"

Bobby's heart stopped as he heard the accusation. His hands shook and his voice trembled as he tried to defend himself. "I wouldn't do anything to hurt you, you know that," he pleaded desperately.

Rosealia grabbed him by the shoulders and shook him furiously. "It could have been anybody. Not just me. Anybody. Don't you understand that?"

Bobby's eyes opened a floodgate of tears. He felt helpless and overwhelmed by her raw anger and pain.

"They're the bad guys, and you're supposed to be smart enough to know that," she said.

"I swear I didn't know anything about it. I don't want anything to do with them. I'm sorry. I'm really sorry."

Rosealia's hands shook as she released her grip on Bobby, her face twisted with anger and betrayal.

Then, Luis' words sliced through the air like a knife, each syllable laced with venom. "Next time, take a better look at who you think your friends are. Good friends do for you... they don't take."

Miguel's body stiffened at Luis' words. He turned back to the window and picked up his hammer, driving a nail that didn't need driving, just to have somewhere to put his hands.

"You never talk to those punks again... ever." Rosealia held out her hand and Bobby immediately understood. He handed over his cellphone.

Luis' eyes narrowed as he scanned the exterior of the house, his attention fixating on the fouled mailbox still dripping. He made his way to the side of the house, where he grabbed a bucket and a sponge. As he filled the bucket with water from the spigot, Bobby reached in to help and the two of them stood holding the handle.

"First, you're gonna tell me where to find them," Luis growled, his voice low and menacing.

Then, without warning, he released his grip on the bucket, the weight of it yanking Bobby off balance and causing him to stumble forward in fear — not for Luis, but for what revealing this information would mean for him once it left his mouth.

That same night, Sanchez was working in his office with Julio logging the day's earnings. Suddenly, a loud crash and bang echoed from the phone room section of the warehouse, followed by shouting. Julio moved to check but was stopped short when Luis burst through the door, his face twisted with anger and intent. Before Julio could react, he was met with a swift punch to the face and locked in a headlock by Luis.

Sanchez quickly grabbed a revolver from his desk drawer and stood pointing it at Luis.

Julio struggled against Luis' hold, but each attempt was met with another sharp blow to the face.

"You're not gonna use that," Luis told Sanchez, whose finger hovered over the trigger as he glared back at Luis. "You don't want to draw attention to your fucking little operation and you'd like an opportunity to fuck with me some more." A sly smile played across Luis' lips as he spoke. "But that one comes with consequences."

Sanchez' grip tightened on the gun as he weighed his options carefully. He knew that killing Luis here and now would only lead to more trouble. He eased the hammer back down.

"If you ever come near my family again, I'll kill you," Luis promised.

WHAM. He slammed Julio in the face one final time for good measure, which caused Julio to melt to the floor, unconscious. Luis then turned and stormed out.

Sanchez slowly sat back down at his desk. Behind him, a credenza ran the length of the wall, its surface lined with framed photographs. He reached back and found the one he wanted — a happy family portrait featuring a man, a woman, and their young daughter with braces on her teeth. He set it down on the desk directly in front of him, and stared at it for a long moment, as his expression hardened into something that had a plan behind it.

CHAPTER SIX
REBUILD OR BURN

The next day at Luis' house, Bobby sat on the front porch steps, miserable and weighed down by his bad choices. He watched as Luis and Miguel stood in the driveway in front of Rosealia's worn-out '57 Chevy Bel Air, their eyes scanning every inch of the car. "We have to tear it down... every nut, bolt and piece of chrome. I'll take care of the engine and running gear," Luis declared.

"I'll start with the body," said Miguel. "This is gonna be so cool. I can see it now... our pictures on the front of Lowrider Magazine! *New Team wins Show. Starts New Business. Life is Good.*"

"That's a long headline," said Luis.

"It's my dream. I'll make the headline as long as I want."

Just then, the low rumble of engines rolled down the street. One truck. Then another.

Luis turned as two pickup trucks eased to the curb, dust lifting around their tires. One new truck sporting a professional sign — *Construction* — and an older one with a spray-painted sign on its tailgate — *Handyman* — the letters uneven, the paint sun-faded. The second one was the kind of truck you'd see outside Home Depot at dawn, with men waiting with tools and hope.

Doors opened. Men climbed out. Tool belts. Ladders. Buckets. Rakes. Someone slid manufactured windows, still wrapped in plastic, from the bed of one truck. Another man hoisted a coil of extension cord over his shoulder like a rope.

Luis stared. So did Bobby and Miguel.

The front door of the house opened. Mama stepped outside, wiping her hands on her apron. She didn't look surprised — she looked ready.

"Buenos días," she called.

The men nodded and smiled, already moving toward the house.

Luis crossed the yard. "Mama," he said softly. "What's going on?"

"They're here to help fix the house."

He frowned. "I don't think we can afford all this."

That made her laugh — not loud, just sure. "Sure, we can," she said. "Because we're not paying."

He looked at the men again.

"They're volunteers," she said.

"Why?"

"Because that's what neighbors do. They don't take. They give."

Something settled in Luis' chest. He said nothing — just smiled.

The house wasn't the only thing being rebuilt. The neighborhood moved like family — quiet, unannounced, bound by something stronger than money.

Luis looked over at Bobby. "Are you gonna get off your ass?" With a heavy sigh, Bobby begrudgingly got up and made his way over to his mom's car.

Miguel grabbed some tools and tossed one to Bobby before they began dismantling the hood. At Miguel's urging, Bobby's movements became quick, sharp, and purposeful as if they were preparing for battle. Luis pulled over an engine hoist.

Parked outside the garage was Miguel's truck with Rosealia's professionally painted sign on the door that read *"L&M Auto — Quality Work at Good Prices"*. Luis and Bobby loaded the engine into it then Luis instructed, "Make sure he knows to call me as soon as it's done, then get right back."

Bobby was actually a safe driver, even though, at his young age, he didn't have that much experience. Nevertheless, he was grateful that Luis entrusted him with this chore. "I will," said Bobby.

"Wait a minute," Mama shouted. As she rushed into the house, she stripped off her apron. A moment later, she returned with her purse. "I need to pick up some stuff."

"Okay, Ma," said Luis.

Bobby stood watching Luis who was thinking. "Is that it?" he asked.

"Yeah."

In all sincerity, Bobby said, "Thanks for letting me..." Before Bobby could finish his thought, Luis gave him a firm pat on the shoulder — a gesture that said, *you're trusted,* without speaking. Bobby then got into the truck and drove off with Mama. Somewhere along the route to the machine shop, unbeknownst to him, Nestor started following, keeping a safe distance.

Luis disappeared back into the depths of the garage, where he worked on the transmission. Meanwhile, Miguel deftly whipped out his pocket knife and sliced through the cardboard box that contained a shiny new alternator. He stood checking the paperwork and specs to make sure it matched what they ordered. Once finished, he turned his attention back to the body of the car, carefully sanding away at rusted patches and imperfections. As they worked, a neighbor approached the open garage door.

"Luis?"

Luis turned and exited. "Al... from down the street, right?"

"Yeah, good memory. Hey, my car's making a funny noise every time I corner it. You think maybe you can fix it... like before five? I really need it bad."

"No problem." Luis put his wrench down, wiped his hands on a rag, and then followed his neighbor to his car. Any paying business needed to be the top priority.

Al glanced over at the work being done on Luis' house. "Ojalá encuentren a los pinches malditos cabrones que hicieron esa mierda," he said---*(I hope they find the fucking bastards who did that shit).*

Luis' expression remained flat, not giving anything away. "Me too."

About an hour later, Bobby pulled up with Mama. They exited the truck, both carrying loads of her sewing work. After dropping off bolts of fabric inside the house, Bobby headed straight to the garage, ready for his next chore, his mood considerably more elevated.

Inside Sanchez' phone room, Julio, with his face bandaged, and Nestor waited anxiously outside Sanchez' office door. As the boss strolled up with two new bodyguards, bigger and tougher than Julio, the duo straightened up. The bodyguards stationed themselves by the door as Sanchez led the way into his office.

Sanchez sat at his large mahogany desk while Julio laid out several thick rolls of cash wrapped in paper and rubber bands. The boss calmly fed the cash through a bill counter and recorded each payment in a thick register before looking up at Nestor with a sharp gaze. "So, what's the story?"

Nestor shifted nervously before answering. "They're building a car for a show. What do you want us to do?"

"Keep eyes on him. Don't do anything until I tell you." With a dismissive wave of his hand, Sanchez went back to counting the money as Nestor and Julio exchanged uneasy glances before quietly leaving the room together.

At midday, Luis and Miguel made their way to the table where Mama had set up lunch in the backyard. Bobby was still working inside.

"Come on kid," hollered Miguel.

"I'll be right there. Just want to get this done," came Bobby's muffled reply from inside.

Rosealia came into the yard and went straight over to Luis, planting a kiss on his cheek. "I dropped off some more supplies for you and Mama. How's it going?"

"Not good," Luis replied with a heavy sigh.

"Why? What's he doing wrong?"

"No. I'm talking about the business."

"Oh. I know it will work out. Just takes a little time. I gotta get back to work." With one last reassuring smile, Rosealia disappeared, headed back to her floral painting job.

Bobby joined them at the outdoor table, collapsing onto a chair with a contented sigh. "I'm starving. What's with that big bag of walnut shells in there?" he asked, gesturing towards the garage.

"For sandblasting your Mom's car," Miguel said.

Baffled, Bobby turned to Luis for clarification. "So the metal doesn't overheat. How we doing on Ramirez' car?" Luis then asked.

"Done," Bobby replied.

"But, nothing else coming in," said Miguel.

"Let's eat up and get back on the Chevy," Luis said, before taking a huge bite of his food, chewing like he could power through the problem.

That night, Miguel walked along his neighborhood streets, alone and bummed out. Things weren't going to be as easy as he had hoped. He peered longingly into the darkened windows of closed shops, seeking some sort of comfort or distraction. And then he saw it — a bar, its neon lights casting a warm glow onto the sidewalk. But it wasn't his usual hangout; he was no longer welcome there. He stood outside for a moment, hands in his pockets, not quite going in, not quite walking away.

A young couple came up the sidewalk behind him, laughing about something, easy with each other, just a normal night out. One of them was hitting a vape pen, and as they passed Miguel the faint sweetness of it drifted back at him — the same kind he'd offered Luis once. The couple pushed through the door without a second thought. The bar's warmth and noise spilled out for just a moment before the door swung shut again.

Miguel's hand was already on it.

He stepped inside, telling himself it was just one drink.

The following day, the Chevy's frame, engine and whatever else were now back from the various car shops. Bobby and Luis stood looking at the engine while Miguel was MIA. "I guess we put everything back together now, huh?" said Bobby.

Luis furrowed his brow. "Did he say anything to you about being late today?"

"Nope," Bobby replied, shaking his head.

Luis moved closer to the engine, inspecting it with a critical eye. "Gimme a hand."

Together, they worked tirelessly throughout the rest of the day without Miguel's help. And as night fell, Luis was still hard at work on the engine, alone in the garage. Exhaustion crept into every muscle of his body, but he refused to give up. That is, until Mama entered the garage. "Luis, I'm going to bed now. You'll have to heat up dinner for yourself."

"Ok, Ma. Have a nice sleep." With gritted determination, he continued working well into the night.

The next day, Bobby found himself outside an auto parts store as part of his chores. He was looking down at his shopping list when Nestor and Joey came up fast beside him.

"Hiya Bobby," said Joey, with false cheeriness.

"Yeah, kid," added Nestor, his tone dripping with malice.

Bobby froze, feeling a knot form in his stomach.

"So where you been? We missed you," continued Joey.

"You wouldn't be working for that scumfuck, would you?" sneered Nestor, referring to Luis.

Bobby tried to sidestep Nestor and enter the store, but they moved with him, effectively blocking his way. In a bold move, Joey snatched the list from Bobby's hands and read it aloud before crumpling it up and shoving it down the front of his pants. They both cackled while Bobby desperately tried to push past them and make his way into the store. He could feel their eyes burning into him as he grabbed the items he remembered from Luis' list. Every time he glanced outside, they were still there, giving him threatening looks. It wasn't until they finally decided they were bored with their own antics that Bobby breathed a sigh of relief. He stepped out of the store and stood a moment on the sidewalk, shoulders tight, jaw set, staring at nothing in particular — just holding it, the way you do when there's no one to tell.

He quickly finished his errand and hurried home, hoping to avoid any more run-ins with Nestor and Joey.

Later, at the garage, despite Miguel's absence the day before, the three of them worked together seamlessly on the engine and running gear. The finished product gleamed with a fresh coat of paint. But as Luis searched for the grease to complete the job, tensions began to rise. "Where's the grease for the bearings?" Luis asked, his tone already frustrated.

"I forgot it," Bobby admitted sheepishly.

Luis let out an exasperated sigh. "Next time I make you a list, read it."

"Sorry." Bobby didn't dare mention his run-in at the store that morning. He didn't want to add fuel to the fire between him and Luis.

By the next day, the car was nearly done. The trio finished putting in the new upholstered seats, then installed a new convertible top.

That night, the men, along with Rosealia and Mama, admired the results of all their hard work and sacrifice. Custom paint and detailing made the car look better than when it rolled off the showroom floor. "Sure is something!" said Rosealia.

"If I knew it was going to look this good, I would have had you fix up the bug first," added Mama.

"The bug's next. I promise," said Luis. "I'm starved. Better be something good on that table."

"What do you think *we've* been doing all day?" said Rosealia.

"All day, huh?" They all smiled and Luis turned off the lights as they headed to the house for a well-deserved meal.

The very next morning, the family and Miguel stood at the curb, dressed in their best clothes and eagerly waiting for Luis to back the Bel Air out of the driveway. The car's sleek exterior shimmered in the morning sunlight.

"But what if something happens to the car before the show?" Bobby asked nervously.

"Have to test drive it," said Miguel.

"Okay, but why do we have to dress up?"

"Tradition," said Miguel.

"Want to look as good as your car don't you?" Mama explained.

That caused Bobby to stand a bit taller and smile.

They all piled into the car, admiring the new car feel, look and smell, before Luis, dressed in his interview jacket, revved the engine and drove off. As they cruised through the neighborhood, heads turned, and eyes widened in admiration at the impressive vehicle. The car seemed to glide effortlessly down the street, leaving behind a trail of envious onlookers.

Luis drove into a parking spot in front of St. Mary's of the Angels Church, honking the horn. Father McGuinn soon emerged from the entrance, his long black robes flapping behind him in the light breeze. With a big smile, the priest approached the car and gave it a thorough once-over. "I think you've got yourselves a real winner here," he proclaimed. Luis and family eagerly piled out of the car, gathering around Father McGuinn as he asked, "When's the big show?"

"In two days," said Luis.

"Excellent! Is everyone ready for a blessing?" asked Father McGuinn, his eyes twinkling with excitement.

A resounding "Yes!" echoed from all members of the family, with Miguel adding enthusiastically, "Bring it on!"

Father McGuinn raised his holy aspergillum and walked around the car, blessing it. He knew enough not to use any holy water as it would have left water spots all over the gleaming exterior, and they would have killed him. "Dear

Lord, bless this car so these good people can win the car show — or at least, place — get lots of customers and come back to church to praise your name. We trust in your good judgment and—"

The sudden roar of a speeding vehicle shattered the moment's tranquility, drawing everyone's attention. They turned in shock to see a massive trash truck barreling toward their position, its horn blaring. They scattered, and in a flash, the truck collided with the side of the Bel Air, pushing it yards away into a concrete wall. It went from car-show ready to a crumpled accordion in a matter of seconds. The impact shook the ground beneath them and two bangers jumped out of the truck and fled over the wall.

As the group rushed to check on each other, they noticed Father McGuinn lying on the ground. He had tripped in his attempt to escape and smashed his head on the pavement. Mama said a quick prayer as the men rushed to his side, except for Bobby, who stood back still in shock, his eyes darting between McGuinn and the damaged car. Rosealia quickly dialed 911 for help.

When Father McGuinn tried to get up, Miguel did his best to comfort him while also restraining him. "He shouldn't move," warned Rosealia.

Luis acted quickly, stuffing his jacket under McGuinn's head as he joined Miguel in keeping him on the ground.

Meanwhile, Mama cried out, "Who would do something like this?"

Luis' jaw hardened as he looked over to the car. His hands clenched into fists, bulging the muscles in his arms, to the point where he wanted to rip off his shirt. "I shoulda taken care of this," he growled. He was just about to get up and stalk towards the car, his mind already coming up with ways to exact revenge, but McGuinn's firm grip on his arm stopped him.

"Don't do it," said the priest. "There's more than one way to win a war." Luis took a deep breath and tried to calm the storm raging inside him.

After the ambulance arrived and Father McGuinn was taken to the hospital, Luis, Rosealia, Mama, Bobby and Miguel returned home. The once lively kitchen table now sat in silence as they each struggled to process what had just happened. Except for Luis, whose fingers tapped the table rapidly, betraying his deep anger and resentment.

"That's it. We're fucked. It's over," Miguel finally said.

"Hey!" Rosealia scolded, causing Miguel to cast an apologetic look to Mama.

"No. He's right," Mama said.

Bobby shifted uncomfortably in his seat, unable to meet anyone's eyes. "It's all my fault this happened," he said. He suddenly jumped up from the table and bolted out of the house.

"Bobby, Bobby... come back," his mother screamed after him. But he kept going as anger and tears filled his face.

"He'll be okay," promised Luis, but Rosealia looked doubtful. Luis then said, "I'll go after him."

Miguel tossed Luis the keys to his truck. "I'll see you tomorrow," he said.

Luis headed outside and scanned the neighborhood, but couldn't spot Bobby anywhere, so he hopped into the truck and took off.

Meanwhile, Bobby trudged past a greasy fast food joint, his shoulders slumped and his head hung low. The familiar scent of fried food wafted towards him, but he had no appetite. He was lost in his own thoughts until a car pulled up next to him. "Hey, kid!" Jimmy called out, but Bobby didn't even look up. Undeterred, Jimmy drove slowly alongside Bobby, matching his pace. "Hey, it's me, Jimmy from the car show. You alright?" Bobby remained silent, so Jimmy pulled into a nearby driveway and blocked Bobby's path. "Get in," he said firmly.

Not long after, Luis happened to drive by and spotted Jimmy's car. He pulled up alongside him and noticed Bobby sitting inside. After a brief exchange, Jimmy said with determination, "I think it's time to call in some favors."

"I can't ask you to get involved," protested Luis.

"You don't have to," replied Jimmy, already making calls on his phone.

Within a short time, they found themselves in a completely different neighborhood. They parked outside an intimidating gang house, where a dozen or so gang members —including the ones from the park — were gathered with their girlfriends, all engaged in wild partying.

The thumping beat of loud music hammered away and could be heard reverberating into the street. The trio approached the door and knocked. Once, twice, louder, then even more incessant. Finally, someone inside heard them, and Julio swung open the door to find Luis, Jimmy, and Bobby standing on the porch. His eyes widened, and a flicker of fear crossed his face at the sight of Luis. But then, glancing back at the crowd behind him, he grinned, confidence returning, and called out. "Well, look who showed up!" Julio sneered, then turned back toward his crew. "The little puta boy... and he brought along a couple of old fart fuckers."

Nestor appeared at the door along with several of his "friends," all eyeing the trio.

"We've got a message for you," said Luis, stepping forward. "Go on, Bobby, tell him."

"I quit," declared Bobby firmly.

"Only dead putas get to quit," yelled Nestor.

Jimmy raised his hand as a signal. On cue, four muscle cars parked on the street suddenly turned on their headlights, aimed directly at the house.

"Tell him the second part of the message," Jimmy instructed.

"If you ever mess with me or my family or any of my friends—"

"You hearing this, cholos... ANY of his friends," said Luis.

Jimmy signaled again, and four more cars joined in, their headlights adding to the blinding glare shining into the house. The bangers squinted in confusion.

"Or even any of my friends' friends," added Bobby.

And finally, four more cars filled the block with an intense glow, drawing the attention of everyone nearby. Confused partygoers came to the door trying to figure out what was happening. The muscle cars revved their engines. Some neighbors ventured out into the street or peered out doors and windows, many wearing pajamas and robes.

The block was lit up like Christmas time.

"All of us." Luis jabbed a finger into Nestor's chest. "Every last fucking one of us. Understand?"

Jimmy then signaled the car drivers to bypass their car mufflers. A deafening crescendo of car engines shook the neighborhood. As Luis, Jimmy, and Bobby walked away, Jimmy signaled the drivers to stop revving and re-engage their mufflers. Slowly, the cars drove off.

"We all stick together...and no one fucks with our cars," said Jimmy, a satisfied smile on his face. Luis simply nodded in agreement.

Bobby turned to Luis with a smirk. "I guess this is one of those rules you were always talking about."

CHAPTER SEVEN

THE PAST DOESN'T STAY BURIED

The next day, the sun was setting as Luis and Miguel returned to the garage, the weight of what they built now in ruins, pressing on them. They began cleaning up the tools and supplies scattered around the shop from working on the Bel Air. "We still got our business. We'll make it," said Luis, trying to inject some optimism into the situation.

"Yeah, we'll make it all right," replied Miguel sarcastically. "Everything will just take a lot longer, that's all. And of course, we have all the time in the world, right?!"

Luis paused to wipe his hands on a rag before turning to face the car in the corner, the one that's been tucked away under wraps for years, like it was waiting for its time.

Miguel, oblivious to Luis' demeanor, kept working. "Fucking cholo punks," he spat out suddenly, breaking Luis out of his trance. He tossed some trash into a nearby barrel before declaring. "I'm outta here," and storming out in frustration.

Luis watched him go before making his way over to the classic Chevy Coupe hidden beneath the tarp. He slowly pulled away the cover to reveal the damage to the front end, hood and windshield of the car. His gaze lingered on the steering wheel for a moment before he finally mustered up the courage to sit behind it. But as soon as his hands touched the familiar leather, memories flooded his mind — ones he tried so hard to forget... not again... not ever. With a shudder running through his entire body, Luis quickly jumped out of the car and slammed the door shut before hastily covering it back up with the tarp, as if he could bury the past with it. He then locked up the garage for the night and the lock clicked like a final word.

Luis walked by Mama's room on his way to the bathroom. When he heard her sobbing, he cracked open the door. She quickly wiped away her tears but Luis entered without asking. "Ma, what's wrong?" He spotted a letter lying at her feet, so he picked it up and read it. He then crouched next to her and comforted her with a hug. "Ah Ma... all the money was from a loan?"

"When I saw you come out of the garage so happy, I had to."

Luis smiled weakly as he thought back to that day. "When was the payment due?"

"Two months ago."

He said nothing for a moment, just stood there holding the letter, the weight of it settling into his hands. Then his breathing went shallow and he set it down on the bureau. "There's no way we're losing this house!"

Early the next morning, Luis stood at the counter of an auto salvage yard office surrounded by stacks of rusted car parts and shelves lined with tools. "They're all from a '57 Bel Air," he told the clerk, gesturing towards the pile of metal parts in front of him. "I can bring in the engine and transmission later if you're interested."

The clerk behind the counter shook his head. "I can't take 'em. I'm sorry," he said, pointing to the already overflowing inventory behind him. "You might try over at Sami's but I think you'll find the same thing. Check the bulletin board. There's a few other places."

Luis let out a heavy sigh as he scanned the cluttered office, hoping for some sort of solution. He then walked over to the bulletin board, took out his phone and took a photo of the list.

At the third shop, a heavyset guy behind the counter didn't even let Luis finish his pitch. "Full up," he said, already turning away, already done with him. Luis stood there a beat longer than he needed to, looking at the parts piled in his arms like they were suddenly heavier than before, then walked back out into the street.

One after another after that, he faced the same wall. The clerk at each shop echoed the same sentiment — they simply did not have the space or need for any more inventory, not even for a bargain.

That night, Luis sat on his bed and once again found himself peering out at the closed-up garage. He leaned back and fell into a troubled sleep that again brought the past to him, to a nightclub, the same nightclub, on a hot summer night some twenty years ago. He was leaving the club, and a younger, drunken Miguel tried to push through the door just as an older, sharply dressed "Salsa Man" with a girlfriend tried to do the same. Miguel and the man exchanged a few heated words, then Miguel and Luis headed toward Luis' classy coupe, which was parked nearby. Miguel, being Miguel, flipped Salsa Man the finger without even turning around. Luis laughed hard at the stupid joke, then flipped off the dude before continuing and turning a corner. But the man wasn't going to let that insult go; he abruptly pushed his girlfriend away and followed after them, eyes cold and locked.

Luis' sleek coupe screamed onto the street, its engine revving with power. Behind him, Salsa Man's car was in hot pursuit, its headlights glaring fiercely. The two vehicles swerved and weaved through the streets, narrowly avoiding collisions, the city blurring into a tunnel of light.

As they approached a short, two-lane bridge, Salsa Man's car suddenly accelerated and passed Luis' car, cutting in front of it. He slammed on the brakes, causing the coupe to veer left into the oncoming lane. The coupe's brakes engaged to avoid an oncoming car. But it fishtailed and skidded towards the other car, narrowly avoiding a head-on collision. Still, it smashed into the driver's side panel, sending both cars careening out of control.

Amidst the chaos, a little girl could be heard crying and screaming from within the oncoming car. She was wearing braces and was in the back seat. As the car broke through the guardrail and plunged off the bridge, flames erupted from the impact. In the coupe, after it came to a stop, vague images flashed by in a blur as a semi-conscious passenger saw arms reaching across from the driver's side to pull him out of harm's way.

Luis jolted awake, heart racing and sweat beading on his forehead. He struggled to clear his head, disoriented in the darkness of his room. As he reached for a shirt, the fabric snagged on the picture of him and Miguel and it crashed to the floor, glass clinking like a warning. In a frenzy, Luis stormed out of his room and down the hallway, awakening his mother with the noise. She emerged from her bedroom only to watch helplessly as Luis thundered out of the house.

Meanwhile, inside his apartment, Miguel was sprawled on the living room floor in a drunken stupor. His back propped against the sofa, he clutched a half-empty liquor bottle and sang off-key to himself. The carpet was strewn with scattered car magazines that he attempted to leaf through in his inebriated state, pages sticking to his sweaty fingers.

Suddenly, a loud pounding on the door barely made Miguel flinch. In his state, he felt giddy and carefree. With a mischievous grin, he straightened himself up before stumbling towards the door and calling out in a high-pitched voice, "Who's calling?" He fell into a fit of laughter at his own joke, then took another swig from the bottle.

"Open the door," came Luis' booming order. Miguel continued laughing as he swung it open, and his friend stormed past him into the room.

"Hey, man, you look like you could use some of this." Miguel offered the bottle.

Luis ignored it and paced. "You know, all this time, since I got out, I've been having these strange dreams and things. And I think it's normal because I see you. I see my mother. I see Father McGuinn. I see Rosie. So, what would you expect, right? I see cars and we talk of shows and on and on. Everything coming back to me." Miguel's gaze darted away, just briefly. "And Lord knows," Luis continued, "I've certainly had those dreams often enough over the years. But tonight. And I don't know why the hell tonight. But I have the same fucking dream except all of a sudden there's something different about it."

Miguel's grip on the whiskey bottle tightened. "I have no idea what the fuck you're talking about."

"They told me back then I might never remember some things about the crash," Luis said, "but I'm beginning to remember what it felt like."

Miguel took a gulp from his bottle, too fast.

"But it feels off. You know what I mean? Like maybe it didn't happen the way I thought it did."

Miguel sobered up instantly. His smile turned to stark fear, and his eyes started tracking every move Luis made.

"You know what I'm talking about, don't you?"

Miguel tried to move away but Luis stuck on him. "No, man, what's to know? You were there," said Miguel, his heart racing as sweat poured down his face.

"I know I was there," Luis snarled. "But now I'm wondering what made you so upset that you tried to kill yourself. Because you thought I lost Rosie? Or was it something else?" He grabbed Miguel by the shirt as if he might strangle him and the bottle fell to the floor.

In desperation, Miguel forcefully pulled away, dropped to the floor, and crawled after his bottle as it rolled and spilled the remainder of its contents across the room. "No, no, no," he howled, tears streaming down his face as he collapsed against the sofa. Miguel clutched the empty bottle to his chest, rocking back and forth in agony. "If they found out I was driving, they would've locked me away for fucking ever. It was last call for me. But you... you were clean. I thought you'd get off."

"Three people died! I'd get off... that's what you thought?!"

Miguel whimpered, covering his ears in a feeble attempt to block out the guilt and shame consuming him. Luis pulled his hands away and screamed. "And a baby girl!"

"I know."

"Seventeen years!"

"I know."

"No, you don't. You'll never know." Luis was about to pulverize his best friend but couldn't bring himself to do it. Instead, he shoved him, and Miguel fell onto his side, curling into a fetal position on the floor.

Luis stormed out and walked the streets. Voices in his head reverberated: *"I thought you'd get off."* ----- *"A baby girl!"* He screamed out, a primal scream, with no one to hear, no one to care. He found himself back at St. Mary's — the same church he had been to so many times before, yet somehow it seemed different now. The little white light bulbs outlining the nameplate flickered on and off like some kind of malicious warning, making Luis hesitate in the doorway before moving away, his feet heavy on the steps.

An abandoned movie theater, its crumbling facade a mere shell of its former grandeur. That's where Rosealia pulled up in her car and parked. She then pushed open a broken door, its hinges creaking in protest, and entered, her feet side-stepping piles of rubble and junk scattered across the floor.

A soft but eerie light partially illuminated the interior from the full moon shining through the decayed roof. Upon hearing a creaking of the floorboards, Luis wanted to leave — every instinct told him to — but the place held him where he sat.

"Luis, you in here? Luis?"

After a moment — "Here."

Rosealia moved toward his voice and found Luis sitting in one of the torn-up seats in a partial row that remained anchored to the flimsy floor that was left. He looked pale and shaken, like he had been scraped raw.

"How did you know I was here?"

"Mama called and said you were acting crazy. She heard a crash then saw you tearing out of the house... then I remembered when you were a kid and upset, you always came here and watched movies all day." Rosealia's tone was gentle as she tried to understand what had brought Luis to this desolate place. She took in the surroundings, noticing that every inch of this once-vibrant theater was now swallowed by shadows and debris. "Remember when they held mass here," Rosealia asked, "while they were building the church?"

Luis smiled faintly. "We couldn't even kneel with all the gum on the floor," he said.

"I got so tired trying to crunch on the edge of my seat pretending to kneel," Rosealia said, "I think my ass still hurts." She laughed softly but there was no response from Luis. "Let me help," she begged.

"You can't."

"What happened?"

He couldn't bring himself to explain; he simply folded his arms across his chest, locking everything inside.

"Hey, what was that science fiction movie you loved? Time something. 'Time Machine', that's it. Yeah, that was good. Weena! I think it was Weena. Gosh, she was so pretty." Rosealia jumped onto Luis' lap. "Let's go."

He stared at her, arms still folded, his body and mind closed off to the world.

"Come on. We're in the Time Machine. We're going back to happy times."

"That's kids' stuff."

"What's wrong with kids' stuff? We can dream can't we?" Rosealia wasn't about to give up. Not now, not after all this time, when there was a chance they'd have a life together after all. She pushed Luis until he couldn't push back, until his breath finally shifted and his arms didn't feel so rigid.

The following day, the sun poured in through the windows as Luis and Rosealia sat at the kitchen table. The smell of freshly brewed coffee filled the room as Mama carefully poured each of them a cup.

"So, what do you think?" he asked.

"A lot of work. But we're used to it. Right, Mama?" said Rosealia.

"Si. But I may have to grow an extra pair of hands."

Bobby entered, looking refreshed, and took a seat. "What are ya talking about?"

"Wanna build another car?" Luis asked.

"What are you gonna use, the bug?" They laughed, except for Mama who said, "You mind what you say about my bug."

Luis pulled out his cellphone and slid it over to Bobby like he was dealing a card in a new game. There in front of him was Luis' photo of the bulletin board. Luis reached over and pinched it wider with his fingers, enlarging the list. Then, with a slow swipe, he shifted the photo to the left, revealing a poster with two fire-breathing beasts, engines flaring and the headline:

Top Fuel Dragsters vs. Funny Cars.
First Ever Sanctioned Showdown!
BIG Cash Prizes & Unmatched Action.

"Funny cars, what the hell are those?" Bobby asked.

"Stripped down, supercharged street cars, built for speed, super light and well, they just look damn funny," Luis explained.

"Everyone's going to help," Rosealia said.

Bobby thought about it a moment longer. "We're building a race car? That's bitchin'!"

Rosealia couldn't help but smile at her son's infectious energy. "He's been hanging around Jimmy too long," she teased, as she got up from the table and approached Luis with a questioning look. "You're really okay with this, right?"

"Yeah, but winning isn't going to be enough. We're really going to have to make a big splash. I have an idea."

CHAPTER EIGHT

THE LION WAKES

By the next day, they had successfully rallied the old gang. The tarp was off the coupe, and Luis, Bobby, Jimmy, Cindi, Mario and Big Huey all wore expressions of anticipation like they were staring down a storm as they looked over the car. "A lot of work," Jimmy commented, whistling low.

Mama crossed her arms confidently. "We're used to it."

"Okay, what do we have and what do we need?" Jimmy asked. "If I remember, you got a 572 under the hood, and as we can see, a supercharger."

"And a Muncie M22 trannny," Luis reminded him.

"It might not be a huge addition," said Jimmy, "but it will definitely help if we add an anti-lag system to make sure that turbo's working 100% of the time."

A high-pitched buzzing suddenly interrupted the group. They turned to see a toy remote-controlled car approach, exhibiting loud clicking sounds, and stop short of the garage door. Behind it was a small boy holding the remote. "You fixed my abuelito's car. Can you fix mine?" he said as he held the remote out in front of him.

Cindi came out of the garage, a sweet smile gracing her lips, picked up the car, and examined it ever so briefly before declaring, "Wow, este es un coche incréble!" Seeing that Cindi was attending to the boy, the men kept assessing the coupe. She put her hand on the boy's shoulder and took the remote from him. "We'll take a good look at it. How about you come back later?" The kid nodded and rushed off, looking back once to make sure his car was indeed in good hands.

Cindi walked back into the garage and put the toy car on the workbench. As she did so, she heard Jimmy say, "It's not enough. It's not even gonna be close. We need more horsepower." Cindi's focus turned back to the toy car.

"Well, I can add another turbo underneath," Luis said.

"Okay, twin charging. Anything else?"

"This is a heavy beast," Mario said, as he slammed his hand onto the fender, "it has to be light as a feather if we're gonna have a chance at crossing the finish line at 340 plus-miles per hour."

"You're the fiberglass expert, so what do you think?" Luis asked.

"I'll hand lay it with lightweight cloth instead of spraying. I'll need help, though." Mario glanced at Big Huey who nodded in agreement. "Great, and I have some vacation days saved up."

"Cindi, did we lose you?" asked Jimmy.

Cindi now turned to the group and grinned as she put down the toy car and waved them over. "Jimmy and I have been working on your idea, Luis. We think we've cracked it." She opened her laptop on the workbench and the screen glow made their faces look younger, hungrier.

The computer screen displayed a rotating wireframe image of the coupe. Everyone gathered around Cindi as she expertly manipulated the image, causing it to morph into something even more impressive — a clean, mean vision of what it could become. Gasps and surprised expressions spread across their faces, quick, involuntary, like the first sparks of a fire catching.

"That looks great but a frame made out of chromoly is very expensive," Luis said.

"Don't worry," said Jimmy. "When the guys hear *El Maestro's* back in the game...you'll have everything you need."

Cindi then added, "Wait, there's more." She rolled the toy car across the workbench. "You want more horsepower? You got it. We swap out the hydraulics with electric actuators that only need a couple of battery packs."

Jimmy's eyes lit up. "You gotta be kidding!" He gave her a big hug then looked over to the others. "They're all doing it now. Aircraft. Robotics. It's all about cutting weight and increasing power. Wait a minute, is that even allowed?"

"I guess we'll find out," said Cindi.

Luis looked around at his dedicated team. "We don't have much time," he stated firmly. "We do this right. We're still standing at the end — people remember that."

That night, the family and crew sat gathered around the kitchen table, plates filled with steaming food. Each person ate with measured movements, lost in their own thoughts and plans for the tasks ahead. Mama's eye caught an empty serving bowl in front of Luis, and without a word, she rose from her seat and headed to the stove to refill it. As she sat back down, she looked around at family and friends alike, grateful for their presence and stubborn enough to believe gratitude could turn into luck.

Early the next morning, the harmonious symphony of work began — metal clinks, wrench turns, the sharp hiss of breath when something fought back. Luis lifted the hood of the coupe and assessed the engine compartment while Bobby scribbled notes on a notepad like a soldier recording orders. The day was filled with a flurry of activity as more work was done on the vintage car. Big Huey emerged from the garage carrying the coupe's heavy hood over his head like the car had already started surrendering to them piece by piece. He carefully placed it on the ground nearby and disappeared back into the garage. Meanwhile, Bobby took inventory of all the parts, making sure nothing was missing because missing one thing meant losing everything.

Amidst the bustle, Jimmy, Cindi, and Mario breezed past Bobby and went straight into the garage where Luis was preparing to remove the engine. With precision and finesse, Big Huey assisted Mario in removing the fenders, doors, and trunk — the coupe slowly shedding its skin. Jimmy meticulously measured for the electric actuators while Cindi entered all the data into her laptop at lightning speed, fingers snapping across keys like she was coding a miracle. It was a well-oiled machine, this team working together to bring new life to the old car. And for the first time since the truck hit the Bel Air, it felt like the world might not deliver the last punch.

It had been a long day. Luis and Bobby were still inside when the others left that night. They passed Miguel who was walking up the driveway, looking worse for wear, his hair unkempt and his clothes rumpled. He was carrying a wooden box that seemed to weigh him down as if it were full of shame, rather than tools. They exchanged glances but said nothing as Miguel kept heading toward the garage. It wasn't their business. All they knew was that there had been a falling out between him and Luis, a large enough one that Luis refused to say a word about it, and they knew enough not to keep prodding him for an answer because the silence around it had teeth.

Luis and Bobby were cleaning and putting tools away when Miguel entered and took in the scene, zeroing in on the coupe. "So you're going through with it, huh?"

"What are you doing here?" Luis demanded, his voice flat, dangerous — like a door being locked.

Miguel shrugged, unsure about everything, and placed the box on the floor at Luis' feet. "I have to sell my tools. Thought maybe you could use them."

Now feeling out of place and uncomfortable with the thick tension between Luis and Miguel, Bobby grabbed the push broom, put his head down, and began sweeping harder than the dirt deserved. Luis ignored the box but kept his gaze fixed on Miguel, as if expecting something more from his long-time friend. But Miguel's betrayal had been too deep; he could barely look Luis in the eyes, and the second he did, he flinched like he'd been struck. Realizing his mistake, he awkwardly picked up the box and turned to leave.

But this wasn't like when Luis was in prison, where he could easily tell some low-life to fuck off or beat the hell out of a guy who did him wrong and be done with it. He and Miguel were supposed to be friends for life, and seeing

Miguel's broken spirit broke Luis' heart anew in a way fists couldn't fix.

After taking a few steps, Miguel heard Luis suddenly speak up, "Bobby, give him the broom." Miguel's breath froze in his lungs and his feet stopped moving. He turned to face Luis. Luis' eyes softened ever so slightly as he watched Bobby hand over the broom like he was handing over a flag instead of a tool. Miguel's strained face lit up with gratitude and relief as he stashed his box under a nearby work table and took over sweeping duties like he'd been given permission to breathe again.

Miguel didn't stop when the floor was clean. He stayed long after Bobby had gone home, wiping down tools, coiling air hoses, and sorting parts that hadn't been touched in years. Luis noticed only because the garage was quieter than usual — the kind of quiet that comes from someone working without needing to be seen. Each day was the same; Miguel doing more than what was expected of him. It was his penance, one that he gladly accepted.

With time of the essence, the crew worked diligently, efficiently and around the clock to meet the looming deadline. The air was thick with the smell of grease and sweat as Luis and Jimmy used the hoist to lift the heavy engine out while

Bobby carefully removed the running boards and tried not to imagine the car failing because of him. Big Huey then loaded the engine into a truck with Miguel at the wheel. Luis, knowing he had to get the ultimate power and torque out of the engine, was sending Miguel to have it blueprinted and balanced. Factory-built engines weren't precise enough; this fine-tuning could help them achieve the edge they needed to win.

At night, Mama entered with her tape measure and took seat cover measurements while the men worked around her like she'd been doing this kind of triage her whole life.

A few days later, at the workbench, Jimmy hooked up a battery pack, and the actuator responded with a quick whine and a series of clicks, as the metal parts moved as designed. Cindi leaned closer and said, "That should do it."

Miguel returned with the engine looking like new and carefully backed the truck into the driveway. He and Big Huey delicately unloaded and hauled the precious cargo into the garage where it would soon be reunited with its home in the car like a new heart being placed back into a body.

Later that night, with Luis and Bobby still working in the garage, Mama sat in the house at an industrial sewing machine making a leather cover for the only seat that mattered —the driver's. Her regular machine, nearby, looked like a toy in comparison. Rosealia walked in. "Work fast, Mama. We only have that machine till tomorrow morning."

Without looking up, Mama replied, "Si, si." She kept up the pace like a speed demon on steroids as if speed alone could ward off bad luck.

When Miguel backed the truck into the driveway the next day, everyone helped unload the coupe's new custom frame.

Cindi worked off the computer model she had made and guided Jimmy as he installed the actuators and battery packs, each placement exact. Luis, Bobby and Big Huey nestled the powerhouse V8 engine and running gear into the frame, keeping everything perfectly aligned.

With just a few days left, Mario backed up his truck to Luis' garage. Bobby eagerly ran out to help unload the fiberglass body parts, his hands moving quickly. As night fell, the entire crew gathered around the coupe, marveling at how it had been fastidiously pieced back together — lighter, meaner, reborn.

The only thing left was a new coat of paint, a task that would fall to Miguel and his skilled spray-painting abilities, as witnessed earlier at Domingo's shop. An enclosed transport truck sat in the driveway, loading ramps lowered and winch ready to receive the coupe.

Luis turned to Miguel. "Alright, Miguel, take the wheel and guide her up, nice and steady."

Miguel's face froze in fear. He quickly held up his trembling hands and stammered, "I... I can't."

Jimmy and his crew were taken aback by Miguel's reluctance since none of them knew the full story of what had happened between Luis and Miguel. Luis placed a reassuring hand on Miguel's shoulder. "Sure you can." Miguel's eyes darted to the others gathered around, feeling embarrassed by his sudden lack of resolve. But then Luis added, "I need you."

The weight of those words sank in for Miguel and he looked back at the rest of the crew. They gave Miguel the final push he needed. Rosealia spoke up first, "We all need you." The others followed with quiet nods and a knowing smile, affirming the truth Miguel needed to hear.

With those final words of encouragement, Miguel mustered up the courage and climbed into the driver's seat. Big Huey activated the winch, and the coupe began its slow ascent, Miguel's focus not wavering. Once loaded, they drove slowly, like the proverbial *Little Old Lady From Pasadena*, to Miguel's previous workplace, where he still had access to a spray booth. There, he painstakingly worked on restoring the coupe to its former glory.

The next evening Luis and Rosealia were standing outside the garage looking in. The coupe was a glossy but unassuming tan bomb — a candy tan with darker-toned pearl top, racing wheels and tires. It looked super slick, like a caramel apple ready for a topping.

"It's all yours," said Luis. Rosealia paused for a moment, studying the coupe's lines the way a sculptor studies stone. She ran her hand lightly along the hood, her eyes narrowing — not admiring the car, but imagining what more it could become. She walked to the workbench, uncovered an array of paints and airbrushes, flipped on the radio and went to work with a focus that shut the whole world out. Luis closed the door as he left her to it.

Early the next morning, Luis opened the garage door, letting in flints of sparkling sunlight. Rosealia was curled up in a ball, asleep on a tarp. He gently scooped her up in his arms, stood looking at her handiwork, and smiled because the car no longer looked like a gamble — it looked like destiny. As he carried her to the house, Rosealia woke up just long enough to say, "All done!" She then fell back asleep again on his shoulder.

The big day had finally arrived. Luis drove the transport truck with Bobby by his side en route to the fairgrounds. Already there, Rosealia waited for her turn at the registration window. The race clerk finished with another registrant then gestured for the next customer. Rosealia hurriedly stepped up and pushed the completed entry form, along with the special waivers required for the electric motors, to him as if sliding in a wager.

The car show area featured a wide variety of custom cars, vans, trucks, and motorcycles, some for display, some for sale. One area was dedicated to the cars racing that day — *Rail Dragsters and Funny Cars* — the type of car category Luis' coupe was in. Tents were set up with lavish displays of auto accessories and clothing. Music filled the air and people were as much a part of the show as the cars themselves. Attractive babes in skimpy outfits. People in period costumes like Zoot suits stood around admiring a group of lowrider cars as if time had cracked open and spilled decades onto the pavement.

Rosealia joined Mama who waited nearby with three small figures, kids who were dressed in mini monk-like outfits, brown robes and with hoods over their heads. "This way, and stay together," Rosealia instructed the "Monks," as she led the group away. The kids looked as if they belonged in a Star Wars movie rather than at a car show, and at least half a dozen onlookers even asked where the Millennium Falcon exhibit was located, as if the day couldn't decide which universe it lived in.

Mama glimpsed a display of outlandishly decked VW Beetles. Rosealia and the Monks were so distracted by the cars and people that they didn't notice Mama was now missing until Rosealia asked, "Where's Mama?" They all looked around frantically. "Maybe she went to the bathroom," Rosealia surmised. She finally spotted her back at the VW exhibit. "There she is. Nobody moves from this spot. That's an order!" The Monks nodded in unison and Rosealia went to get Mama, fighting her way through the crowd and around the car displays, elbowing through perfume, exhaust, and adrenaline.

But the Monks soon spotted a huge bicycle display and off they went. They broke into a run, their little robes flailing, and ended up at the Schwinn bicycles exhibit displaying elaborate gold-plated chains, fancy jewel-tone-painted frames, some with jeweled steering wheels instead of handlebars, custom seats, saddlebags and crystal-adorned baskets. They could barely contain themselves like the whole place was made of shiny temptation. Pint-sized owners, with their parents, proudly stood by as the Monks walked around, their little hands pointing.

Mama stood mesmerized at the VWs as Rosealia arrived. "Mama, you shouldn't walk away like that. You'll get lost."

"Look!" she said, pointing. "It looks like my car."

"Mama, they all look like your car... well, not exactly."

"That one! It's got the same little flower vase near the window, see?"

Rosealia glanced at the rose-filled vase on the passenger side of a candy red bug with gleaming gold accessories. "Very nice. Now, come on, we gotta go." She ushered Mama away before Mama decided to adopt the thing and never leave.

"I want Luis to hurry up and fix up my bug."

"Right after they win." Rosealia caught up to the Monks, who were still in thrall of the bicycles, and steered everyone toward the competition like herding cats through a carnival.

In the drag strip area, owners and mechanics made final preparations on two dozen cars. The coupe wasn't one of them. Jimmy, Cindi, Mario and Big Huey waited anxiously as Rosealia, Mama and the Monks arrived, and every minute felt like a brick added to their chests.

"Where the hell are they?" Rosealia asked, looking for Luis' truck.

"I thought you knew," said Jimmy. "They sure left in enough time to get here before us."

"Yeah, they did," said Rosealia, but the words sounded thinner than she wanted.

They all looked off in the distance toward the entrance gate as the Race Announcer said, "Attention everyone. The first race starts in ten minutes. I understand we're waiting for one more entry to arrive. Let's hope they make it."

"Please God," said Mama, as she pulled out her Rosary Beads and made the sign of the cross fast.

"Shit," said Cindi, "maybe they hit traffic. We should go look for them."

"They won't get here any faster if it's traffic," reminded Jimmy.

"Well, it could be something else. Maybe it's a flat tire."

"I'll call Bobby," said Rosealia. She opened her purse and realized she had two phones. "Oh, no, I still have Bobby's phone. Let me call Luis." She dialed quickly only to have it go to voicemail.

"All right. Come on, guys," Jimmy said as he, Mario and Big Huey disappeared into the crowds.

On the freeway, Luis and Bobby were stopped in traffic. "Better call your mom and tell her."

"I'll have to use your phone," said Bobby.

Luis dug his phone out of his pocket and handed it to Bobby.

"Passcode?"

"1234," said Luis, which elicited a chuckle from Bobby.

"What?"

"You know you have to charge this thing, right?"

"Of course."

"Well, it's dead."

Bobby glanced in the side view mirror and spotted Nestor's car. "Maybe we should get off the freeway," Bobby said, keeping his voice flat so it wouldn't crack.

"Yeah, I've been thinking about it."

"Now would be good."

Luis saw Bobby looking in the mirror. He glanced in his own side mirror and spotted Nestor's car trying to keep up, so he pulled into the right emergency lane and sped to the next exit. Nestor's car followed fast behind. The two vehicles sped along, weaving in and out of traffic, turn signals forgotten, reaching surface streets where Luis made a sharp right as a traffic light changed from yellow to red. Nestor was about to follow but he spotted a cop car and quickly came to a stop. Pedestrians crossed in front of him, and for a split second, Luis thought they'd lost him.

Luis now found himself stuck at a crosswalk behind a few cars waiting for show-goers to cross. He could see the brightly lit fairgrounds just a few blocks away, beckoning him. He drummed his fingers restlessly on the steering wheel, growing more impatient by the second. "To hell with this." Suddenly, he slammed his foot on the gas pedal and swerved into an alley, narrowly missing a couple of pedestrians, their shouts chasing him like thrown rocks. But as he drove through the narrow passage, adrenaline coursing through his veins, he was met with an unexpected obstacle. Nestor's car slowly drove by, then backed up quickly, blocking Luis' path. Luis threw his truck into reverse and attempted to back up, but another car, with Julio and Sanchez, was right behind him, two intimidating goons, already spilling out like a trap. They exited their car and moved toward the truck, brandishing bats, sledgehammers, and chains, ready to unleash their fury upon Luis, metal scraping the pavement as they walked.

As he stepped out of the truck, Luis gave Bobby a quick command: "Lock the doors." Bobby's hands shook as he obeyed, feeling trapped and helpless in the tense situation unfolding before him.

Jimmy patrolled the streets, his eyes scanning for any signs of Luis. As he turned a corner, he immediately recognized Luis' waylaid truck parked in the alleyway, boxed in like a stray. No pause, he pulled in behind Nestor's car, blocking their exit.

Sanchez stood at the front of Luis' truck, flanked by his goons and other bangers from Nestor's car, as they closed in on Luis. Bobby sat inside the truck, trembling with fear, but he knew he couldn't just sit by and do nothing. He rushed out of the truck and yelled defiantly at Sanchez, "I'm not going back to your fucking gang," his voice breaking through the alley like glass.

Sanchez let out a roar of laughter as his men joined in. As he turned to Bobby, Sanchez' face twisted into a grotesque mask of rage. "You think this is about you, you little shit?!" He then turned to Luis and pointed. "I'm here for him."

As Jimmy and Mario approached the scene, they were armed with tire irons while Big Huey hauled a car jack behind him like some prehistoric brute dragging a weapon toward battle, his massive frame bent forward with purpose. The air was thick with tension as everyone prepared for a fight, the kind of stillness that comes right before a storm.

Luis' gaze burned with fury as it locked onto Sanchez. "You and me, let's do it."

Sanchez scoffed. "That would be too easy. You're gonna keep suffering just like I have to every day."

Confusion crossed Luis' face as he looked around at the surrounding threat. He threw his hands up in frustration. "What the fuck is your problem?"

Sanchez' eyes darkened as he spoke, his voice dripping with malice. "Remember the bridge? The car that went over? That was my brother and his family, you fuck, and I've been waiting...all this time...just for you."

A wave of realization crashed over Luis. But before he could process it further, the sound of fists meeting flesh brought him back to reality. Big Huey took on two of Sanchez' henchmen while Luis, Jimmy, and Mario brawled with the others. Bodies collided and metal weapons clanged together, echoing off brick and dumpsters.

Sanchez stood back, his eyes gleaming with sadistic pleasure as he watched every blow land on Luis, savoring it like a meal. But then suddenly, the truck's back door began to slowly inch up, revealing a small gap of only a couple of feet. Miguel emerged from the truck, taking advantage of the distraction and sneaking up behind Sanchez and pressing a knife against his throat. "Tell them to stop," he commanded in a low voice filled with deadly intent.

Sanchez didn't move.

"I'll cut your fucking throat. I have nothing to lose."

Sanchez, feeling the blade dig in, yelled, "Stop... stop!"

All eyes were on Miguel as he held the knife firmly against Sanchez' throat. "Make them drop their weapons," he said.

Sanchez gestured to his goons, who hesitantly lowered their weapons, chains sagging to the ground, bats clinking.

"He didn't kill anybody. It was me," Miguel admitted, "I was driving the car." The weight of the admission hung heavy in the air as Miguel's words pierced through the tense silence. Now everyone knew the truth — even the bangers who didn't care suddenly did. He turned to look at Luis, his eyes brimming with remorse. "Go on, Luis," he pleaded, "get out of here." But Luis, instead, took a step toward Miguel, as if closing a distance could change a past. "You know I've got to do this," Miguel explained, hoping to make Luis understand that he had a lot to make up for.

Suddenly, the shrill wail of police sirens shattered the moment, drawing everyone's attention to the source. Some pedestrians had spotted the melee and called it in. A small crowd formed at the alley's entrance, their eyes fixed on the unfolding scene with curiosity and fear, phones up, faces pale.

Luis gave a curt nod to Miguel. Then he turned to Jimmy and Mario, their expressions mirroring his own resolve. It was time to get the hell out of there before things got any worse. Big Huey had his goons in headlocks, one under each massive arm. The muscles in his biceps bulged as he squeezed until they dropped, melting into the pavement like butter, wheezing and coughing.

Jimmy leaped into his car while Big Huey followed Mario, who jumped into Nestor's car, and both vehicles backed up rapidly, tires screeching against the pavement, as they made their escape from the alley. Luis' truck rumbled behind them, its engine straining, as it joined the other cars in their hasty retreat, threading through streets like a needle.

Just as they were all far enough away to let out a sigh of relief, flashing lights and sirens cut through the air. Cop cars appeared on the scene, turning into the alley just moments after the group had made their getaway, too late to see anything but dust.

In the truck, Luis rolled his neck once and set his jaw. Whatever had just happened in that alley was done. The coupe was in the back. The fairgrounds were three blocks away. He floored it.

Back at the fairgrounds, Rosealia, Mama, Cindi and the Monks sat in the bleachers, agitated and just about holding their breath, hoping Luis would make it in time. Two cars that just finished racing headed back to the staging area.

"And there you have it! The rail car takes the win, proving once again the raw power and speed of these top-fuel machines! A nice round of applause for Dale Marion. We have just one more race to go." People cheered and applauded for Dale's good fortune.

Cindi's heart leapt as she caught sight of Luis' truck and Jimmy's car pulling into the grounds. The sound of the truck's horn blared, announcing their arrival to the rest of the crowd. The excited chatter and anticipation filled the air as people made way for the vehicles to pass. Mama and Rosealia finally exhaled a sigh of relief, knowing that all members of their team had safely arrived.

As Luis' truck made its way towards the staging area, Cindi noticed Luis' cut lip and felt a twinge of worry. But her nerves were soon put at ease as Jimmy and Mario rolled up the back door of the truck, revealing darkness within, then the first glint of tan paint. Despite their bruises, they didn't waste any time getting to work. Bobby and Big Huey assisted in unloading the two wheel ramps while Jimmy directed the positioning of the coupe, snapping orders like a pit boss.

With bated breaths, everyone watched as the coupe's engine roared to life, causing the ground to shake beneath their feet. Slowly but surely, the front end of the car descended the ramp, revealing its expertly painted exterior. A lion's fierce face adorned the hood, its nose serving as the hood ornament, while its mouth was cleverly painted onto the grill. The car's fenders proudly displayed massive lion paws, adding to the overall ferocity of the design, a full-on predator emerging from the shadowed cavern of the transport.

As onlookers pushed forward, curious and awed, laughter erupted throughout the crowd. A few good old boys sneered dismissively at the spectacle before them.

"What the hell?"

"Should be in the display area."

"Shoot it!"

Luis drove the coupe past the spectators to the starting line, eyes forward, jaw set.

"Well, I don't know why this car owner has gone seriously rogue, but okay, I guess. No rules against wildlife on the track. Good luck," bellowed the announcer, riding the crowd like a wave.

A sleek, devilish black rail car with *"Black Magic"* emblazoned in red on its side pulled up next to Luis. The driver grinned at the wildlife, then gave Luis a welcoming nod, like he could already smell an easy win.

Jimmy, Bobby and Big Huey joined Rosealia, Mama, Cindi and the Monks in the bleachers. Sitting behind them were friends from the neighborhood. Cindi noticed Jimmy's bruised face and was shocked. "What happened to you and where the hell's Miguel?"

"Tell ya later."

"Come on, let's go up," said Rosealia. She, Jimmy and Cindi walked up to the announcer's table where he was ready to start the race. "Let's get ready to—"

Jimmy whispered something to the announcer.

"Just a minute folks. You all know Jimmy and Cindi Randiker."

Some people from the crowd yelled—

"We love you Jimmy!"

"Cindi! You're the best."

"We love you too," said Cindi. "Listen everyone, we just want you to know that the coupe in front of you is here not because of big money sponsors, but because of the hard work and love of friends and family, and because some people refuse to stay down."

"So, please, please give them a big muscle car welcome!" Jimmy shouted.

All the spectators in the stands rose to their feet, cheering loudly and showing their admiration. Some even let out lion-like guttural sounds of approval, half joking, half meaning it.

"One more thing," said Cindi. "Hit it, Rosie."

Rosealia's eyes sparkled with excitement as she pressed the play button on her cell phone and held it up to the announcer's microphone. The familiar tune of *Wimoweh: The*

Lion Sleeps Tonight blasted through the loudspeakers, causing a surge of energy among the audience. In an instant, the Monks burst onto a platform, throwing off their dark robes in dramatic fashion. It was the girls from the church choir, clad in short tan velour outfits adorned with long brown tails and matching furry headbands resembling manes. As they began to sing and dance, their movements were fluid and cat-like, perfectly synchronized to the beat of the music, goofy and brave at the same time.

Cindi got the crowd going. It was so kooky that people joined in clapping and stomping to the music. As one of the girls hit the notes: *Oooohhh, Oooohhh, Oooohhhh, Ooooohhh* .... a low growl came from the car. And as the growl grew, people now paid attention to the coupe, the way a room goes quiet when something unexpected happens. The front of the car lowered while its back end raised up as if turning into a cat ready to pounce. When the back end finished raising, steel chrome spikes, simulating claws, extended from the paw-like fenders.

The crowd became so boisterous that people rushed in from other areas to watch.

Then, with a massive roar, the back of the car fell to its original position. Cheers and applause filled the air, and the announcer called out, "Let's get ready to rumble!"

The deafening roar of engines reverberated through the air as the two cars lined up side by side at the starting line.

Their chassis shimmered under the harsh sun, reflecting the countless hours of labor that had gone into crafting these beasts of speed and steel.

To the left was 'Black Magic,' its metallic black paint gleaming brilliantly with intricate streaks of lightning dancing along its sides. To the right sat the 'Coupe,' a sharp contrast in lion-hued caramel; its claws and fangs made it look as if the machine were already tearing through the jungle, even while stationary on the track.

The atmosphere was thick with tension and anticipation. Spectators leaned in, eyes trained on the two racers, eager to witness this clash of pro versus newcomer.

As the moments ticked toward the race's start, the drivers methodically began their pre-race rituals.

Black Magic's driver revved the engine a few times, feeling the raw power rumbling beneath. He pushed forward the first gear lever, and the rear tires began to spin, quickly enveloping the back of the dragster in thick white smoke. This 'burnout' wasn't just for show — it was crucial for heating up the tires, ensuring they'd have maximum grip once the race began. Inside the cockpit, the driver's right foot gently feathered the gas pedal, while his hand rested on the first gear lever, feeling the engine's readiness through every vibration.

With his left foot on the clutch and right foot on the gas, Luis initiated the Coupe's own burnout, matching the energy of his rival. The pungent scent of burnt rubber intertwined with the thick smoke, becoming an almost tangible sign of the impending race.

The whine and growl of both engines were a symphony of power, a song known and loved by all drag racing aficionados.

With burnouts complete, both cars crept forward towards the staging beams. As the front tires broke the first beam, the pre-stage bulbs lit up on the 'Christmas Tree' — the vertical sequence of lights that signal the start of a race. With a few more inches forward, the stage lights illuminated, signaling that the dragsters were in position and ready. The palpable tension was now almost unbearable. All eyes were fixed on the Christmas Tree, waiting for the sequence: Amber... Amber... Amber...

And then, with an explosive burst of energy, GREEN.

As they launched, the rail car driver stayed in gear and floored the throttle, while Luis released the clutch and hit the gas. When it came time to shift into second gear, the rail car driver smoothly moved his hand to the next paddle, locking it in place. Luis expertly manipulated the clutch and gas pedal, his hands and feet moving in perfect harmony, a flash of precision and speed. This sequence repeated for each gear, showcasing the distinct launch styles of both drivers.

The dragsters, with raw power unleashed, left nothing behind but scorched asphalt and a trail of exhilarated screams from the crowd. The quarter-mile showdown had begun.

The cars thundered down the tarmac, engines howling in a relentless crescendo, embodying the very essence of speed. Like twin bolts of lightning, they zipped along, each inch they covered only amplifying the heart-pounding thrill of the chase. Luis, gripping the wheel of the Coupe, his knuckles white with tension, danced on the edge of machine capability and human instinct. Every twist of the wheel, every fractional throttle adjustment, was a testament to his sheer determination to overcome Black Magic.

The Coupe and Black Magic traded leads, neither willing to relent. Each car surged and retreated, a mesmerizing dance of power, precision, and sheer will.

Luis' eyes bore into the track, every ounce of his strength and savvy at play, keeping the Coupe from becoming a mere shadow under Black Magic's might. His breaths were sharp, rapid, in tune with the pulsating rhythm of the race.

As the finish line loomed, both machines gave it their all, their engines screaming in harmonious defiance. And then, in a final burst of speed and roaring engines, they crossed the line, parachutes blossomed open, reeling them in with a dramatic deceleration, their positions so close that uncertainty hung in the air. Silence enveloped the dragstrip, the crowd collectively holding its breath. The outcome? An agonizingly suspenseful photo finish, the kind that makes even the most stoic forget to blink.

As the cars rolled back to the staging area, the crowd buzzed with excitement, awaiting the results. The announcer paused, a hint of suspense in his voice. "Just a moment, we need to check the replay," he said, conferring with the race officials. The spectators' anticipation intensified, growing more restless with each passing moment. And finally, the announcement: "It's a tie. I can't believe it. In all my years, I've never seen a funny car match a rail car. And, it's the fastest time of the day!"

The crowd erupted in cheers and admiration of the great feat, with some chanting *Wimoweh, Wimoweh, Wimoweh*, like they had been waiting their whole lives to say it.

Luis and the other driver stepped onto the trophy platform and raised the first-place prize together. Luis' smile broadened as he motioned for Rosealia, Mama and his friends to join him as photographers snapped away when the group gathered around, banged up and grinning like they owned the day.

The announcer shushed the crowd to report another big surprise. "I've just been notified by the sponsor of Black Magic that all the prize money will go to Luis Alvarez and his crew for a spectacularly wild show and a great finish. So, congratulations one and all, and that is class, folks."

The accolades went on for some time, with the group fielding questions from the crowd and basking in the attention. Cindi handed out her business cards; Jimmy explained the work they had done on incorporating electric motors; Rosealia gave out lion-faced button cards for her artwork business. Mama sat in the bleachers with Bobby, the Monks, Mario and Big Huey all taking a load off, finally letting their shoulders relax.

In time, life's rhythm found its way back to the garage, the tools, the people who showed up.

Rosealia strolled up to a modest industrial unit brimming with vehicles, each eagerly awaiting its turn for repair or restoration. *L&M Auto* read the newly installed sign. She breezed in carrying a large paper bag, the smell of lunch cutting through oil and metal. Tucked away in the corner was the coupe, its familiar silhouette no longer shielded by its tarpaulin veil, now a symbol of healing and renewal.

Amidst the clinking tools and the hum of machinery, Luis and Bobby were deep in their work with a customer's car. Rosealia set up lunch on the table inside the little break room. "Time to eat!"

With that, the symphony of the garage paused. Tools were laid to rest, and as the men washed up, Luis threw a glance back, asking, "You coming?" A moment later, Miguel slid out from under a car, the glint of his ankle monitor catching the overhead lights. He'd told the truth to the police that night in the alley. What came after was between him and the law, and he accepted every condition without complaint. His face lit up in a grin, a man paying his debt and still showing up, and together, the band of brothers made their way to the break room.

Left behind in the garage, a solitary carburetor rested atop a thick newspaper smeared with sordid tales and heavy grease. The bold headline screamed, "Local Businessman Convicted of Racketeering," right beneath a photo of the infamous Sanchez, eyes dead on the page. Hovering above the workbench, like a guardian of cherished memories, was the gleaming drag race trophy. Beside it, a large framed photo painted a story of love and unity — the coupe poised regally outside the church, with Luis, dapper in a rented tux, and the radiant Rosealia in a modest, off-white gown. They were encircled by a tapestry of loved ones — Mama, Bobby, Miguel, Father McGuinn, and a crowd of friends, all donning attire befitting the momentous day, and for once, nobody was running.

THE END

AUTHORS

J Bartell, M.A., is an author, screenwriter, and behavior specialist, renowned for developing and teaching his process known as 'Left-Right Brain Suggestibility.' He was previously a licensed Marriage, Family, and Child Counselor in California. In his mid-thirties, J became Chief of Staff at one of the world's largest therapeutic/educational institutes. At that time, he gave lectures and live demonstrations of Pain, Bleeding, and Muscle Control at UCLA and other venues. His clients included people from all walks of life, but it was his worldwide travels on behalf of affluent, private individuals, including heads-of-state, that put him on the radar of the CIA. For more information about J, visit his website at http://jbartell.com.

Ginger Marin is an actor, author, screenwriter, and animal rights advocate. As a former network TV Journalist at NBC News NY, Ginger served as producer and writer for the network's top news shows and various special reports. She is also the author of "Monster on Mars" and "Adventures in Avalon: An Offbeat & Quirky Adult Bedtime Story". To learn more about Ginger's acting and film projects, visit her IMDB page at http://www.imdb.me/gingermarin or her personal website https://gingermarin.com. If you want to read how she bemoans the world, check out her blog at http://bioniclady.com